CRIMES AND CHIMICHANGAS

A Mexican Café Cozy Mystery

Holly Plum

Copyright © 2017 by Holly Plum

All rights reserved. No part of this publication may be reproduced, stored in or introduced into a retrieval system, or transmitted, in any form, or by any means (electronic, mechanical, photocopying, recording, or otherwise) without the prior written permission of the copyright owner of this book.

This is a work of fiction. Names, characters, places, brands, media, and incidents are either the product of the author's imagination or are used fictitiously. Any resemblance to actual persons, living or dead, business establishments, events, or locales is entirely coincidental.

CHAPTER ONE

"Of course it's only a start-up company, but you wouldn't believe how many investors we've gotten since I started working here six months ago." Mari's childhood friend, Jemina Little, talked with her hands. "Turns out, there are a *lot* of wealthy Texans looking to throw money around."

Jemina led a group of visitors through the halls of a rented building on the east end of town. Among the visitors was thirty-something-year-old Mari Ramirez and her mother, Paula. Mari's tiny bulldog, Tabasco, trotted at her feet.

"Will the company keep making dog treats or will they be branching out into other things?" Mari asked casually. She ran her fingers through her brunette bob.

Jemina, who was wearing a well-tailored skirt suit and heels, smiled and pointed at Mari as if she had been expecting her to ask the question.

"It's entirely possible that Woofles Snack Company might eventually branch out," Jemina stated. "But for now, we're just having fun selling our signature maple bacon flavored dog treats shaped like miniature waffles. The response has been unbelievable."

She spoke every word in an incredulous tone as if even she couldn't believe her good fortune. It reminded Mari of her uncle who had once won the lottery. He had spoken just like that until he lost all of his winnings buying wizard memorabilia.

"But you don't even like dogs, Jemina," Mrs. Ramirez pointed out.

Jemina raised a finger to her lips and winked conspiratorially.

"My boss doesn't need to know that," she whispered.

Mari turned to look at her mother. She shook her head, and Tabasco barked. This was Jemina's first time leading a tour group, and Mari knew how much Jemina's job meant to her. By now the little group had reached the end of the hallway and stood in front of a pair of white double doors.

"We're just here for support, remember?" Mari muttered.

"Before we go in," Jemina announced, "I would like to thank Mari, Paula, and the entire Ramirez family for offering to cater the opening of our new division. Y'all are our first official group to have a look at our local facilities. Lito Bueno's Mexican Restaurant is the best Mexican restaurant in town—"

"It is the only Mexican restaurant in town," Mari and her mother said in unison.

"Thank you," Jemina repeated.

There was a smattering of applause, and the Ramirez women bowed modestly.

Jemina pushed open the double doors and led them into the conference room. It was a large remodeled room with floor-to-ceiling windows looking out over the desolate remains of what had once been a thriving industrial center. Even from the opposite end of the room, Mari saw train tracks and an abandoned shopping center. It wasn't a pretty sight, but it was a reminder that the Woofles Snack Company was attempting to revive the surrounding area.

Tables with appetizers and drinks had been set up along the empty walls. Together the small party made its way to the edge of the room, where a crowd of employees was already gathered and sampling Mari's bite-sized chimichangas.

"Now, you made sure the menu was completely nut-free, right?" Mari asked as she poured lemon-lime soda into a clear plastic cup.

"I did," Mrs. Ramirez replied, sipping her drink with a distracted look on her face. "Mari, why did Jemina agree to work for this start-up if she hates dogs?"

"She doesn't *hate* them," Mari said, placing the cap back on the bottle with a twist. "She just doesn't like them."

"And yet she's agreed to let Tabasco be a taste-tester." Paula raised her eyebrows as she observed the food trays from a distance. "Looks like we're getting low on tortillas."

"Which Tabasco is very glad to do." Mari leaned back against the table and took a sip of her drink. It was cold and fizzy. "But the reason she took a job at Woofles is because she wanted to move back home and help take care of her mom."

Mari understood Jemina's decision because she too had recently left a full-time teaching job in Fort Worth to return home and work at Lito Bueno's Mexican Restaurant, her family's legacy.

"Hey, pretty lady," said a man who stood at the end of the buffet table carrying a plate full of chimichangas. He wore a navy blue three-piece suit, a pair of designer sunglasses atop his head, and an expensive looking watch. Mari was so distracted by his appearance that it took her a moment to realize he was talking to her.

"Excuse me?" she said.

"Yeah, you," he said, biting into his food as he looked her up and down. "Now that I know this is the view at Lito Bueno's, I will have to go there more often."

"Right," Mari responded, grabbing her mother by the arm and moving toward the center of the room. "Enjoy your food, sir." But as they were walking, Mrs. Ramirez noticed her own mother standing near the doorway. Paula tugged at Mari's sleeve.

"What is your Abuela doing here?" Paula asked.

"I didn't even know she was coming." Mari shrugged. "Did you invite her?"

"Keep an eye on the drinks. I'm going to go find out what this is about." Mrs. Ramirez left Mari standing there to monitor the entire buffet.

Because Mari's brothers had neglected to set out enough tables and chairs, people were forced to stand and eat. Mari wandered through the crowd, eyeing plate after plate of her Tex-Mex appetizers. To her great relief, the smarmy young man was gone. As she snatched a handful of chips from the buffet, Jemina came striding over accompanied by a man and woman who looked as if they were in their mid-twenties.

"Well, I think he's just awful," the woman finished saying. She had on bubblegum pink heels but not the bubbly expression to match.

"He *is* awful," the man next to her agreed. "And also… charming?" He laughed and nudged her gently in the ribs, but she did not look entertained.

"Mari, I'd like you to meet my friends Andre and Yvette," Jemina introduced the pair. Andre shook her hand enthusiastically while Yvette gave a curt nod.

Mari had a feeling she knew who they had been talking about.

"Who was that man?" she whispered as she glanced over her shoulder. "The man in the three-piece suit?"

"That's my boss," Jemina replied, looking worried.

"*Our* boss," Andre added, motioning to himself and Yvette and chuckling.

"His name is Dale Roberts." Jemina rolled her eyes. "Did he say anything to you? He has the tendency to make inappropriate comments at work. But no one ever says anything to him because…well, he is the boss."

Each of the three leaned forward with interest and listened as Mari recounted meeting him.

"I got the distinct impression he was hitting on me," Mari muttered.

"Of course he was," Andre said. "That's just how he rolls. He doesn't mean anything by it. I would be surprised if he's even interested in you at all."

"It's his way of asserting dominance," Yvette commented. "But it's still awful, and I wish he wouldn't do it. One of these days he's going to get sued."

Jemina gave a wary glance in Tabasco's direction, who was kneeling obediently at Mari's heels. She folded her arms crossly. "I don't care whether he means it or not. It's creepy. I don't like being hit on when I'm working. I get my fair share of weirdos at the restaurant."

"I've never dared ask him, of course, but I have a feeling the only reason I got this job was because of my looks." Jemina shrugged. She and her coworker Yvette were very pretty in Mari's opinion.

Andre raised his eyebrows.

"That couldn't have been the only reason," he said. "Surely, you had an excellent resume."

"And a hot bod?" Jemina added jokingly. "Don't answer that, Andre."

The argument might have gone on for some time if Dale Roberts hadn't chosen that moment to interrupt.

"Can I have everyone's attention?" Dale announced, hitting the side of a plastic cup with a plastic fork. It didn't make as much noise as he'd expected. "Darn. That didn't work so well. Note to self. Next time, splurge for the glassware, am I right?"

Mari rolled her eyes at his joke, but the rest of the room laughed.

"Here he goes," Yvette muttered. "He loves to brag."

"You might have thought you were all coming out here to celebrate the success of Woofles Snack Company," he went on. "And it's true that the last six months have been amazingly successful. We have satisfied the maple bacon-flavored dog treat needs of our customers with the press of a button."

Setting his plate down on the floor, Dale picked up the cup again and raised it into the air as if making a toast.

"Someone just get him a champagne glass before he goes on whining again," Yvette said lowly.

Jemina nodded. "I already checked the break room."

"But that's not the real reason I invited you all here today," Dale added. "The truth is that I gathered you all here because I wanted to make a special announcement."

There was a murmur of surprise from the crowd gathered around him, and Dale waved his arms as if calling for silence. But it was only when Mari saw the panicked look on his face that she realized he was having trouble breathing.

"What's wrong with him?" Mrs. Ramirez asked, appearing beside her daughter.

Dale didn't say another word. Instead, he fell to the floor.

"He might be having an allergic reaction," said Jemina. Despite what she had said about her boss earlier, she looked worried.

"Is he the one who's allergic to nuts?" Mari asked. Jemina had asked her to serve a nut-free menu for the sake of one person in the office, though she hadn't specified who. "Does he have an epi-pen?"

Jemina was about to answer when Yvette interrupted.

"There should be one in his office," Yvette stated. "Top drawer of his desk. Dale's office is down the hall. It's the third door on the left."

Propelled by a sense of urgency, Mari raced down the hall toward Dale's office. She pulled out every drawer in his desk but found only a chaotic assembly of pens, sticky pads, safety pins, and loose staples.

"It has to be in here somewhere," she said aloud. "Come on." After sifting twice through the pile on the floor, her heart sank. There was no epi-pen in Dale's office. And if there was, it had been moved or hidden somewhere out of sight.

Mari panicked, not knowing what to do next.

The door to Dale's office burst open, and Jemina entered looking deathly white. "There's no easy way to say this, but it's too late."

"What do you mean?" Mari replied. "Is an ambulance here already?"

"One is on the way," Jemina informed her. "But..."

"What?" Mari's eyes went wide as she purposefully avoided the logic of the situation. She didn't want to admit to herself what had really happened. "Just say it, Jemina."

"He's gone." Jemina gulped. "My boss is dead."

CHAPTER TWO

"Dead?" Mari said, finding the truth difficult to swallow. "Are you sure?"

Jemina nodded gravely. "I went ahead and called the police."

She spoke these last words quietly and then paused as she silently stared at the floor. Mari felt cold all over. She sat down on the floor to prevent herself falling over from the shock.

"I swear to you I didn't use nuts in *any* of the food," she said, breaking a silence that had threatened to go on indefinitely.

"I believe you," Jemina replied, joining her on the floor. "Unfortunately, I think this accident wasn't an accident at all."

"You think Dale was—"

"Murdered," Jemina finished. "Maybe. Let me ask you this. Where's his epi-pen?"

"I wasn't able to find it," Mari answered.

Jemina leaned in close and whispered. "Exactly."

Mari was shaken, and her mind raced with theory after theory about what happened to Jemina's boss. Jemina shook her head. Mari hoped that she was wrong and that Dale's death was just a horrible accident. If Jemina were right, she and Mari would most likely be suspects in a murder investigation. Especially Mari since her family's restaurant had catered the food.

"What happened after I left?" Mari asked. For the moment she thought it best not to let Jemina know of her worries.

"Panic," Jemina responded. "He fell face forward onto the carpet. Your dog ran over and tried to lick his face. Everyone was yelling and crowding around him."

"And you think this happened on purpose?"

"The fact that you couldn't find his epi-pen is suspicious. He *always* kept an epi-pen in his desk, along with a backup one. Always. With an allergy like his, he didn't take chances."

Jemina glanced shiftily around as she said this. Mari couldn't help but feel that she might have been hiding something. "I see."

"He was always prepared for an emergency like this one," Jemina continued. "I mean, you saw what just happened. He used to say he couldn't

15

even be in the same room as a peanut. It was just a joke, but there was obviously some truth to it."

"Okay, but it couldn't have been the food," Mari assured her. "Mamá and I made the food, and we both knew somebody in your office had a bad nut allergy. We took extra caution."

"I know you did," Jemina replied. "I'm not accusing you of anything, Mari. You're an old friend of mine. I think the food was tampered with."

"By who?" Mari's heart pounded as she considered the possibility.

"The same person who stole Dale's epi-pen."

Mari looked at her skeptically. "You seem to have thought this through quite a bit."

Jemina shrugged her thin shoulders. "I read a lot of Nancy Drew when I was younger. I guess I've always sort of imagined myself as a detective."

"Yes, I remember the notebook you carried around in grade school," Mari commented. "But that room was filled with people. How could someone have tampered with the food without anyone noticing? My eyes were on the food most of the day."

"I don't know." Jemina sighed. "I know it's a stretch, but someone clearly found a way. I'm going to need your help to figure this out."

"Why do you need my help?" Mari asked. She hesitated to get involved, but she couldn't say no to helping an old friend like Jemina.

Jemina drew a deep breath as she began composing herself to rejoin the crowd.

"Because," she said, "my boss has just been murdered. I'm pretty sure someone local did it. Maybe even someone in my office."

"I hope you are wrong," Mari replied.

"I might be working with a killer, Mari. And I have no idea what the killer is after or what he, or she, might do next."

As the two women made their way back to the conference room, the body of Dale Roberts was being carried out on a stretcher. The rest of the assembled guests looked on in silence. Mrs. Ramirez had her arm around Mari's grandmother. Lito Bueno's Mexican Restaurant was about to be linked to another murder investigation.

After a quick search, Mari found Tabasco lurking under a folding table. He whined as she tried to pull him out from under it.

"You're coming with me," Mari whispered, grabbing him gently by the legs. "You're going to help me interview witnesses."

***

The first witness Mari interviewed was Yvette, who stood at a window near the back of the conference room. She drew her jacket tight around herself when Mari approached as if wanting to be left alone to grieve in solitude.

"Awful, isn't it?" Mari attempted a conversation, letting Tabasco break the ice by allowing him to sit at her feet.

Yvette sniffed loudly. Mari was surprised to see a single tear trickling down her cheek.

"I've never seen someone die before," she said in a shaky voice. "I've been to funerals, but that's different. The person you are going to pay your respects to is already gone at that point."

Yvette broke off as if hating herself for admitting that she had been moved by her boss's death. She tried to compose herself by straightening her shoulders and forcing a blank expression.

"It was a shock to everyone," Mari commented.

"He was such a jerk, especially to me," Yvette blurted out. "And then he had to go on and die like he did. Now, I feel sorry for the guy. I hate that I feel sorry for him."

Mari raised her eyebrows, a little confused. She quickly gave Yvette a reassuring pat on the shoulder as she processed her comments. Below them, a train rumbled as it passed the building. The sound of the engine was the perfect white noise to cover up the awkward silence. Mari thought carefully about what she should say next. Tabasco playfully licked Yvette's shoe.

"Earlier," Mari began, "you mentioned something about Dale being sued."

"Oh, right," Yvette said. "That wasn't a far-fetched comment. He already has been sued multiple times. I suppose now that he's dead I won't get in trouble for speaking the truth."

"For what?"

"What do you think?" Yvette looked at Mari as if the answer were obvious. "Sexual harassment, of course. But the same thing happens every time. Either the woman has no proof, or any witnesses mysteriously decide not to talk."

"Strange," Mari responded.

"Not really." Yvette sniffed, almost completely back to her old self. "He was loaded. Men like that do as they please. Until one day it all comes back to bite them."

"So you don't think what happened to him was an accident?" Mari's eyes went wide as she eagerly waited for answers.

"We'll know soon enough," she replied quietly.

Tabasco barked, and Mari hurriedly changed the subject.

"I wonder what his big announcement was all about," Mari added. "Any ideas?"

Yvette nodded. "I'm pretty sure he was about to name Andre the new Marketing Director."

"Really?"

"He mentioned it last week," Yvette admitted, clenching her jaw in frustration." Both Andre and I were up for the position, and Dale told me he was giving it to Andre. No surprise there. Like he ever would have given that sort of promotion to a woman."

"I'm sorry to hear that."

"Don't be sorry," Yvette insisted. "The game just changed." She stared out the window again. "Oh, look. More policemen are here."

CHAPTER THREE

Each guest hung around the building as the police questioned everyone. It was clear that Dale Roberts had made a few enemies. Mari wondered if the guy had any redeeming traits because what she had learned about him so far wasn't promising. Any number of his employees, including Yvette, had a motive for wanting Dale out of the picture.

Mari turned to the one employee she had yet to speak to. One that actually had positive things to say about the deceased the last time she had spoken to him. Mari found Andre leaning against a wall in a secluded corner of the conference room. He was eyeing his drink uneasily as if hoping that it would magically turn into a way for him to leave.

"I'm sorry for your loss," Mari said, not knowing how else to broach the subject. Out of the corner of her eye, she saw her mother and her Abuela deep in conversation. No doubt they were worried about being blamed for adding nuts to a nut-free recipe.

"This wasn't how I expected this meeting to end," Andre responded.

"I take it you and Dale were really close."

"Yeah, if you can ever really be *close* to your employer," Dale answered. "I wouldn't say we were best friends, exactly. I wanted to be his friend. I hope that's how he saw me, as a friend."

"Well, you must have known him outside of work, right? That would count as a friendship I would think." Mari couldn't help feeling that she was pushing her luck with the questions, but if she didn't ask she would never know.

"We did, on occasion." Andre took a sip of his drink. The pained look on his face suggested that he found it distasteful. "We went golfing together sometimes. He was an excellent golfer, although, honestly, not as good as he thought he was. He was much better at drinking."

There was more than a touch of sadness in Andre's laughter.

"He did seem to have a high opinion of himself," Mari said. Her gaze darted to the window as a red Cadillac pulled into the parking lot.

Andre glanced at Mari suspiciously. Mari thought he was going to scold her for speaking so callously of his former boss, but to her surprise, he nodded in agreement.

"That was one of the delightful things about him, I thought. It grated on some of the others, the women especially. They just didn't understand him like I did."

"Understand what?" Mari asked.

"That was just his style." Andre grinned. "Dale wasn't conceited or narcissistic, just self-promoting. He had a healthy view of himself. It was one of the qualities that made him such a successful businessman. A lot of people complained about it, but none of those people were as driven or motivated as he was. None of them shared his success."

Andre launched into a short speech about the envy that those without ambition always feel toward successful people. Mari pretended to listen patiently, but out of the corner of her eye, she saw her Abuela exiting the room. Mari's mother followed her.

"I get it." Mari tried to cut her conversation with Andre short. "He was successful."

"Oh, no question," Andre responded without hesitation. "He had an incredible talent stack."

"Talent stack?"

"You know how some people are insanely good at doing one thing?" Andre explained. "Dale wasn't one of those people. He was decently good at four or five different things. He was effortlessly charismatic, had a good head for business, knew how to handle the press; he knew how to promote his brand. If you put all that together, you have an unstoppable businessman. He was brilliant."

Mari had long been able to hide her true feelings when interviewing potential suspects, but she couldn't help being impressed by Andre's fervor for his ex-boss. He spoke of him the way a man might toast a beloved friend at a wedding reception. Mari had spent several years working for her father, but even she would have been hard-pressed to muster that level of enthusiasm for a guy like Dale Roberts.

"You are the first person to say such *nice* things about him." Mari took a deep breath and glanced down at Tabasco.

Andre gripped his cup tightly. "Yeah, he was just—so great. He was my mentor in a way."

"He must have thought highly of you, too," Mari added. "I heard you were due for a promotion."

Andre couldn't conceal the disappointment on his face as Mari brought up the subject.

"I was, actually," he admitted. "That's what this whole meeting was about. He promoted me to Marketing Director. A huge honor."

"I got the sense that some of your co-workers weren't too happy about it."

"Well, *they* can get over it," Andre said. "And by *they* I mean Yvette."

***

After the police were through, Mari returned home for the evening. She brewed herself a cup of tea and sat at the kitchen table trying to figure out who had the best reason to kill Dale Roberts.

Although she had found his remarks toward her unprofessional and off-putting, Mari had been moved by the admiration he seemed to inspire even in those who disliked him. While she thought it unlikely that Andre would have killed him, she had an equally hard time believing that Jemina might have done it. The grief she had demonstrated over his death was genuine, and she seemed to have been as surprised as anyone else when he sank to the floor for the last time.

"I don't know what I'm going to do," Mari said to Tabasco, who was seated a few feet away tearing into a package of Woofles dog treats. "This guy seemed to have pissed a lot of people off, but I don't have many leads. And I know that *I* didn't do it. We've got to figure something out before the police decide to blame this all on the family restaurant."

Of course, she still didn't know for sure whether or not Dale had really been murdered. Perhaps she was jumping to conclusions and the events of the day were just one big freak accident. Or maybe Jemina had fed her the idea of murder. Mari had seen many murder mystery shows in which the culprit had killed one person and then framed another. Was Jemina, Yvette, Andre, or someone else from the office trying to frame a coworker for the murder of Dale Roberts? Might his death have been a tragic accident that one of his employees was now using to enact some kind of revenge?

There was no way to tell. Mari stayed up half the night trying to figure it out with little success. In the meantime, Tabasco had great success as he finished off his package of maple bacon flavored dog treats.

CHAPTER FOUR

The next morning was chillier than usual for the quiet Texas town that Mari called home. When she arrived at work a few minutes before opening with her bulldog Tabasco, her jacket was covered in raindrops. She hung her jacket up to dry on the coat rack next to the front entrance when a figure appeared right behind her. Tabasco barked, and Mari jumped. She was relieved to see that it was a familiar face.

But she was worried by the fact that it was Detective Price.

As usual, the town's detective was wearing a dress shirt and tie that didn't match too well. The detective nodded, knowing the Ramirez family for their breakfast burritos, which he ordered regularly, and their penchant for attracting trouble. The detective smiled at Tabasco, and the dog trotted off to his usual spot in the back office of the restaurant.

"We've still got a few minutes before we open for lunch," Mari said. "How can I help you this morning, Detective?"

"I want to talk to you about the death of Dale Roberts," he responded, following her to a booth near the kitchen where they both sat down. "As you may have already guessed, his death is extremely suspicious. I haven't spoken to the press yet, so this stays between you and me, but at the moment we're treating this as a murder investigation."

Mari nodded as if she had been expecting this. "May I ask why?"

"A number of reasons," the detective explained. "Many of which I intend to keep private for now."

"You're here to ask me about the food," Mari guessed.

Yes, of course." He pulled a notebook from his pocket and began jotting things down.

Mari proceeded to explain how Jemina had asked her to cater the food for the event but had asked her to prepare a menu without nuts.

"Did she explain why?" Detective Price asked.

Mari shook her head. "Just that someone in the office had an allergy. She didn't say who, and I honestly didn't know it was Dale until he went into shock. I swear there were no nuts on the buffet table."

"What was on the final menu?"

"Oh, the works," Mari replied. "Rice, beans, chips and salsa made with our secret family recipe, guacamole, a burrito bar, my bite-sized chimichangas—"

"And did you happen to notice what Mr. Roberts was eating before he died?"

"I caught a glimpse of his plate," Mari admitted. "It was stacked with chimichangas, which isn't unusual. They are a huge crowd-pleaser. If he ate anything else, I didn't notice it."

"Who made the food?" he continued to question her.

Mari scratched her head. She was beginning to feel anxious, as she always did whenever Detective Price served up a rapid-fire serving of questions. She took a deep breath, hoping that the murder investigation wouldn't go on for long.

She could only hope.

"Mom and I cooked all of it." Mari cleared her throat. The truth didn't make her look less guilty. "And my Abuela made the tortillas for the burrito bar. She makes them better than anyone else, and she insisted on it."

"And you're one-hundred percent sure none of the food contained nuts." The detective raised his eyebrows.

Mari nodded. "I double ... no, I *triple* checked. We take special orders very seriously around here."

At that moment Mari heard the familiar chime indicating that a customer had entered the restaurant.

"I can wait while you tend to customers," the detective said.

A second later Mari's mother and grandmother came into the dining room, both bundled up in their thickest white coats and looking oddly like marshmallows. Her Abuela went straight into the kitchen while Mrs. Ramirez joined Mari and the detective in the booth. She rubbed her hands vigorously as if the cool weather outside were a brisk snowstorm.

"You wouldn't believe how cold it's getting out there," Paula Ramirez commented. "I don't know how they do it in the Midwest."

"They are used to it," Mari responded. The last time it had come close to snowing was ten years ago. In Mari's tiny hometown, drivers had panicked and left their cars sitting in the middle of

31

the street. Every school and business had also shut down in the ensuing chaos.

"I was just talking to Mari about yesterday," Detective Price informed her. "I understand you ladies did the catering."

"We double ... no, *triple* checked that there were not nuts in the buffet," Mrs. Ramirez stated, anticipating his question. Abuela came walking out of the kitchen with a mug of hot chocolate and sat down next to Mari.

"And when did you arrive at the party?" Detective Price asked.

"We got there at a quarter to five?" Paula looked to Mari, who nodded. Mari's grandmother spoke some words in Spanish, which Mrs. Ramirez translated. Policemen made Abuela nervous. "Abuela didn't show up until a little later."

"Why is that?"

Mari shrugged

"Abuela came with a friend from her sewing club," Paula answered for her mother.

Detective Price paused and ruffled his hair in agitation. It was clear he didn't want to ask his next question. Mari froze, suspecting that she wouldn't want to answer it.

"I've already told Mari," he said, "and please keep this between us, that I'm working under the assumption that Dale Roberts was murdered. Now I need to know if either of you left the food unattended at the party."

Mari thought hard about it.

"I wasn't at the buffet table the entire time," she admitted. "There was a moment when I stepped outside with Tabasco. I didn't want him making a mess on the carpet. Jemina was using him as a taste-tester, and he had way too many treats."

"How long were you gone?" the detective asked.

"Five to ten minutes," Mari guessed.

Detective Price turned to Mrs. Ramirez. "And did you step away from the food, Mrs. Ramirez?"

Paula nodded. "I was supposed to be supervising, but I did leave once ... or twice."

"Where did you go?"

"I took a few phone calls in the hallway," Paula answered.

"Mamá," Mari muttered.

"What?" Paula shrugged. "You how your father gets when I don't return his calls." She turned to Detective Price. "I got my husband one of those new touch screen phones for Christmas, and now my inbox is overloaded with emojis."

"So there was a window of opportunity," Mari said quietly as she thought of Dale's seemingly well-known nut allergy.

Paula's phone began buzzing, and she held up a finger. "Excuse me for a minute," she said as she left the table.

Detective Price returned the pencil and notepad to his coat pocket. "I suspect the food could have been tampered with while either you were outside, Mari, or your mother was on the phone."

"But how is that possible? There were always people around. Surely someone would have noticed." Mari shook her head.

"Do you always notice what's happening around you?" the detective asked. He turned and pointed to a table on the opposite end of the room. "You didn't even notice when that woman came in."

For the first time, Mari saw that there was a woman seated at the table near the window. It was the woman her grandmother had driven home with the night before. Mari's jaw fell as she realized how little she had been paying attention. Abuela looked at the woman and waved at her to join them.

"Good day to you both," the detective said, putting on his hat and walking toward the front door.

Tabasco came running through the restaurant. Mari's father, José Ramirez, followed with a look of concern on his face. Without bothering to acknowledge the departing detective, Mr. Ramirez walked straight to the booth where Mari and her grandmother were sitting.

"Family meeting in my office in three minutes," he said by way of greeting. "We have an extremely serious issue to discuss."

CHAPTER FIVE

Mari, her mother, and her grandmother gathered in the back office of the family's restaurant. Mrs. Ramirez made a pot of coffee while Mr. Ramirez tried to stop Tabasco from pulling up a stray piece of carpet.

"What did you want to see us about?" Mari asked, intervening to rescue her dog before her father ushered him out of the room with his foot.

Mr. Ramirez straightened up, took a cigarette out of his shirt pocket, and placed it in his mouth without lighting it. His wife knocked it out of his hand with a scowl. She had been trying to get him to quit for years.

"Oh no you don't, José," Paula scolded him. "You have enough health problems as it is."

José took a deep breath and cleared his throat as he handed his wife the carton of cigarettes.

"What I'm about to say doesn't leave this room," Mr. Ramirez said. Mari felt an immediate sense of déjà vu. "I need to know if any of you has been taking money from the register."

There was a swift and collective gasp among them.

"Of course not," Mrs. Ramirez replied, nearly rising out of her seat. "That you would even suggest such a thing—"

Mr. Ramirez motioned for her to sit down. "Okay, I didn't think so. That's all I needed to hear."

But Mari wasn't willing to let it go at this. "You're saying that someone *has* been stealing money from the till," she asked. "What makes you so sure?"

She quickly thought about everyone she knew who worked at the restaurant and might have had access to the register. There were her two brothers, Alex and David. Although they had gotten into their fair share of trouble, Mari didn't think they were dumb enough to take money from right under their dad's nose. Chrissy, the waitress, was an equally unlikely suspect. She had been working at the restaurant for years.

"For the last week, the register has been short twenty dollars at closing," Mr. Ramirez replied. "It can't be a coincidence. A crime has been committed."

None of the women spoke for a moment. The fiery look on her father's face worried Mari.

He was often grumpy, but seldom upset like this. The fact that he had been able to remain relatively calm and composed until now somehow unnerved her even more.

"I'm going to figure out who is doing this, and losing their job will be the least of their worries," he continued. "I'm going to press charges. I've already spoken to the police, but I need each of you to keep an eye out. Let me know the moment you see anything suspicious."

Mari couldn't decide whether it was the thefts or the murder that seemed to be drawing every officer in Texas to Lito Bueno's Mexican restaurant for lunch that afternoon. They had all insisted that they were only there to eat lunch, but Mari knew better. Officer Rick Kinney, with whom she had once shared a memorable date, sat in a corner booth with his jug ears attuned to the conversations around him.

"You'll be having your usual, right?" Mari said, trying and failing to hide a playful smile. "Beef enchiladas, double rice, no beans, and a side of green chili?"

"To-go if you don't mind," Rick replied, ruffling his dark hair shyly. "But for here I would like a plate of your bite-sized chimichangas."

Mari rolled her eyes and snatched his menu. Once she had placed his order, she came back and sat down in the seat opposite him.

"So," Mari said coyly, "I wanted to talk to you about something."

Officer Rick knew Mari well enough by now to know what she was up to.

"We don't have any leads on the investigation yet," he stated. "It hasn't even been a full day. But I'll let you know when we come across something."

"That's not what I was going to ask," Mari lied.

"Really?" Rick raised his eyebrows. "You weren't going to ask me anything at the incident that happened at Woofles Snack Company?"

"Okay, fine I was," she admitted. "But that's not all." Mari proceeded to tell him about the money that had gone missing, hoping that his experience might point her in the direction of the culprit. "My dad will let this drive him crazy until he figures out what happened to the money."

"Well, if he thinks someone working here is stealing there are ways to find out for sure," Rick responded.

"Like what?" Mari asked.

"A simple lie detector test." He grinned smugly.

Mari exhaled loudly. "You want me to hook every employee up to a lie detector? That will go over well."

"No." Rick shook his head as if the solution were obvious. "I mean you can ask your employees test questions to see if they lie to you."

"Can you teach me?"

"I can't train you to read people over lunch," Rick answered. "But I can give you some pointers. You know how in the movies when a person is lying they get all nervous and fidgety?"

"Yeah," Mari responded. "Isn't that a classic sign that someone is hiding something?"

"Yes and no." Rick clasped his hands together and leaned forward. "Actually, the opposite is more likely to be the case. See, a lot of folks are aware of what a lying person is supposed to look like, so they over-compensate. They make extra sure that you believe their lie."

"But how can I tell if someone is nervous or just overly chatty by nature?"

"The trick is to watch their eyes," Rick replied. "Do they avoid looking at you? Do they look at you too much? Do their eyes dart around the room? Observe how someone behaves in a normal scenario and then watch for the differences when you bring up the money."

"Oh, brilliant." Mari took a deep breath. "It's that simple, huh?"

Mari decided to try these techniques on the rest of her coworkers during her shift that afternoon. She questioned Chrissy and Mateo the bus boy about their lives outside of work. Mateo, in particular, was notoriously secretive, though Mari could never figure out why. But if Chrissy or Mateo were lying, they were either doing a remarkably good job of it, or she was just terrible at catching them at it.

Mari was still testing out her new methods when Jemina showed up after her shift for drinks and dessert.

"How are things at the office?" Mari asked, squinting hard as if trying to read Jemina's mind.

Looking vaguely uncomfortable, Jemina responded, "Now that the initial shock has worn off, no one is that upset about Dale's death. Except for Andre, obviously. He took half the day off work, and the other half he spent coming up with theory after theory as to who will be taking over the company. I think he's worried that he won't be getting his promotion."

"That poor guy," Mari said.

"Andre was always quick to defend Dale, no matter how boorish he was being. He didn't believe the rest of us when we told him about all of the sexual harassment stuff."

"Have the police been in to question you again?" Mari went on.

"Several times." Jemina held up her drink before taking a swig. "It was hard to get anything done with that Detective Price hanging around. But I did some digging of my own, and you won't believe what I found."

"An answer to all of our problems?" Mari chuckled, taking a bite of the fried ice cream she'd brought out from the kitchen.

"When I went looking through Dale's office I found a list of all his businesses and properties. Apparently, he was trying to buy the place across the street—the Lucky Noodle."

"No way." Mari's jaw dropped. She had known Mr. Chun and his daughter, Jia, for years. He and her father had a rivalry that dated back to before she was born. Mr. Chun had pulled trick after trick to steal customers, sometimes going as far as trying to release rats into the kitchen.

"Yeah," Jemina continued. "I guess having some success with dog food made him think he could become a restaurateur. And it appears that Dale offered the owner a huge sum of money for it."

"I wonder why Mr. Chun turned it down," Mari replied.

"I don't know, but I would like to find out." Jemina rose from the table grinning, a tenacious look in her eyes. "Wouldn't you?"

CHAPTER SIX

The Lucky Noodle stood directly across the street from Lito Bueno's Mexican Restaurant. It had been there for nearly thirty years. Mr. Ramirez and Mr. Chun had been at each other's throats for about that long as well. Mari could remember when she was a little girl, watching them fight from behind her mother's legs.

Mari would never admit it out loud, but she loved the smell of the food. The stir-fried vegetables and fried egg rolls wafted through the room as she opened the door. Unfortunately, if she wanted to spare her father the heart attack, she couldn't be seen eating anything from Mr. Chun's menu.

Mr. Chun knew that Mari and her brothers hadn't inherited their father's reflexive hostility towards him and his business. At one point Mari's little brother Alex had even dated Mr. Chun's daughter. So, Mr. Chun was willing to talk to her whenever she came in with questions. On this particular evening, however, the restaurant was unusually crowded.

"Not now, Mari," Mr. Chun said bluntly. "My customers come first."

As he said this, a young man wearing a beige fedora jostled past Mari, hitting her hard in the elbow.

"Hey, come back here," Mr. Chun shouted. "You can't cut in line. You have to wait to be seated."

"I know your hands are full, but this will only take a minute." Mari followed Mr. Chun around the restaurant as he served customers.

"Please, will you help us?" Jemina cut in. "I am a customer. I was in here last week, remember? The number five special for one."

Mari watched as Mr. Chun's face visibly softened when he heard the pleading tone in Jemina's voice. Mari made a mental note to congratulate Jemina later on her excellent acting. It wasn't *lying*, exactly, but it was something close.

"Come with me," Mr. Chun said with a reluctant sigh. "Both of you."

Motioning for Jia to cover the register, he led Mari and Jemina into his office. It was the mirror image of her father's office, except that it faced the other way and an antique bronze tea kettle had taken the place of the coffee pot.

"So, as you might have heard," Jemina said, "my boss, Dale Roberts, died yesterday afternoon."

Mr. Chun looked confused. "Is that a fact? Well, I am sorry but what has that got to do with me?"

"More than you think," Jemina said. "We think he might have been murdered. And, to be honest with you, so do the police. We don't think you had anything to do with it, but we think he may have tried to contact you shortly before he was killed."

As before, Mari marveled at Jemina's gift for talking to people. She had a way of engaging them, getting their attention, and finding out exactly what she needed to do to get what she wanted. It occurred to her that Jemina would have made an excellent detective herself.

"What makes you think he contacted me?" Mr. Chun asked without bothering to deny it.

Jemina told him about how she had seen his name and business listed among the properties Dale planned to buy.

"It's true," Mr. Chun confessed. Mari nearly gasped. In her previous interviews with him, it sometimes took him an hour to stop being stubborn and answer her questions. "There was a time when my business wasn't doing as well as it is now. Back then, Dale offered to buy The Lucky

Noodle, and I seriously considered selling it to him."

"Why didn't you?" Mari couldn't help asking.

"Because what he wanted for this place was not what I wanted for it. I wasn't going to leave it in the hands of a man who disrespected it. I might as well sell it to your father."

Ignoring the slur on her father, Mari said, "What did he want to do with it?"

"He wanted to turn it into a take-out only place," Mr. Chun replied with a look of disgust. "He wanted to cut out half the menu and serve sushi. The nerve of that man."

"Well, you have a great restaurant," Jemina responded. "I am glad you didn't sell."

"So am I," Mr. Chun said. "I'm sad to hear of Dale's death, but I'm not sad about my decision. Besides, he had plenty of other investments. He didn't need mine."

Mari and Jemina raced back across the street toward Lito Bueno's Mexican Restaurant feeling exhilarated by their success.

"Did you see that?" Jemina commented looking pleased with herself. "Can you believe he opened up to us like that?"

Mari shook her head in disbelief. "I've never seen him talk to anyone like that. You sure have a way with words."

Mari avoided the suspicious glances of her father as she sat at a booth in the corner with Jemina. Mari asked Chrissy for two of Abuela's hot chocolates and a basket of warm sopapillas.

"I'm betting Mr. Chun wasn't the only person who refused to sell Dale their business," Jemina continued. "But we're still so far from having a motive."

"That leaves us with your coworkers," Mari suggested. "There is plenty of motive among the women at the office."

"That is true," Jemina replied. "Luckily he never got handsy with me."

Chrissy placed Mari's order on the table, and Mari took a sip of her drink.

"Of course, we can't overlook Andre either." Mari savored the rich chocolaty flavor that delighted her taste buds. "He is so adamant that he and Dale were buddies that I wonder if his grief is—"

"Just an act?" Jemina guessed.

She nodded. "I didn't want to say it, but yeah."

48

"It's impossible to tell when Andre is acting. He brings the same level of enthusiasm to meetings as he does to making coffee in the morning. It can be a bit much.'"

"I should talk to him again," Mari added. "Maybe his story will change."

Jemina stayed until her hot chocolate was gone. After Jemina had left, Mari returned to the kitchen as she thought through what she and Jemina had discussed. She found her grandmother standing at the stove warming tortillas in a cast-iron skillet.

"You know you don't have to keep doing that," Mari said. "It's late. You can go home for the night."

"I know," Abuela said in Spanish. "I find it relaxing. Besides, your father is driving me as soon as he finishes the accounts. Renata's knee is acting up again."

"Renata?" Mari repeated.

"My friend Renata from sewing club," Abuela replied, not looking up from her cooking. "The woman you saw in the dining room this morning. She has been driving me to meetings."

"Funny," Mari went on. "I don't think you've ever mentioned her before."

49

"We met at church last Christmas during the nativity pageant. She invited me to her sewing club, and we've been friends ever since." Abuela fidgeted with the spatula in her hand. It wasn't like her to avoid eye contact during a conversation. When Alex and David did it, she had always scolded them for their bad manners.

For the first time that day, Mari had the distinct feeling she was being lied to.

CHAPTER SEVEN

The next morning, Mari attempted to take Tabasco for a walk. The sky was gray, and the ground was damp from a rain storm that had passed by through the night. Most of the joggers and dog-walkers she was used to seeing on her morning strolls hadn't even bothered leaving the house. Mari was left alone with her thoughts, and the sound of Tabasco's growls every time a bird flew by.

Mari's cell phone buzzed in her pocket, and she scrambled to answer it. She hoped it was Detective Price calling to tell her that the culprit had been caught, but she knew it was probably too soon for that.

"Yes, this is Mari," she answered hopefully.

"Mari, I have some urgent business to discuss with you," the detective said before she could even say hello. "Our tests have just come back from the lab, and it appears that there was peanut powder in your chimichangas."

"I'm not going to pretend that I'm surprised," Mari replied, watching Tabasco chase a small squirrel that scurried away with an annoyed look. "I figured that something strange was going on. I can assure you though that I did not add peanut powder to *anything*, and neither did my mother."

"At the moment the fact that you never met Dale Roberts until the day he died is working in your favor," Detective Price said. "So now the question becomes who did it?"

Mari had no answer. After she had finished walking Tabasco, she decided to visit Woofles Snack Company and continue trying out the techniques she had learned from Officer Rick. Maybe she would stumble across a disgruntled employee with something to hide.

"It's the least I can do, you know," she told Tabasco. "Someone has got to keep the police from thinking me or anyone else in the family was involved in this death."

Tabasco barked in agreement as he jumped in the car. The two of them drove to see Jemina at work. Tabasco barked as they entered the parking lot, sniffing the air to his heart's content. Mari wasn't at all surprised that Tabasco had seemed to memorize the factory's location. He wagged his tail all the way inside the office building.

The shock of Dale's passing must have worn off because the office was bustling. Not many people had the time to greet Mari or Tabasco, and no one was pleased by Mari's questions.

"I want you to think carefully before you answer," Mari said as she stood in the break room with Yvette, Jemina, and Andre. "Did any of you see someone standing near the food doing anything that looked suspicious?"

Yvette and Andre both shook their heads.

"I had to chase your dog away from the table a couple of times," Yvette said in a resentful tone, brushing her hair back behind her ears. "No people, though."

Mari turned to Andre, who looked flustered. "I wasn't really paying attention. I was too busy thinking about my upcoming promotion."

Yvette glared at him, annoyed. Mari suspected this wasn't the first time he had brought up his promotion since Dale's death. But she also had an inexplicable feeling that Yvette and Andre were both lying about something. Andre avoided eye contact, and Yvette was overdoing it.

Mari was still eyeing them both thoughtfully when the door of the break room opened, and a petite, frizzy-haired woman Mari recognized as Dale's secretary came in.

"I wasn't sure who to tell," the woman said timidly. "But there's a woman here claiming to be Dale's sister, and she wants to speak with one of you."

Andre clapped his hands enthusiastically. "Show her in, please. I will handle this."

A young woman with a mass of curly blonde hair came walking into the room. In spite of the gloomy conditions outside, she was wearing a thin pair of slacks and a blue blazer that was only half-buttoned.

"I'm June," she said. "I was wondering if someone would show me to my brother's old office."

She didn't bother to specify why she needed to see his office, so Mari followed at a close distance while Andre led her down the hall. The whole way there he was talkative, asking her where she was from and telling her he had once gone surfing in California where his family owned a summer home. Jemina walked alongside Mari, rolling her eyes.

"Sounds great," June said. "I don't have much time for the beach."

"Well, you are missing out," Andre responded.

"You sound like my brother. I assume you're into sports as well?"

"Extreme sports," Andre exaggerated. "Skiing, rock climbing, anything involving a parachute—"

"Seriously, Andre?" Jemina muttered. "Watching that window washer last week made you uncomfortable. You're afraid of heights."

Andre's neck stiffened as he glared at Jemina.

"Jemina, don't you and your friend have somewhere to be?" Andre continued. He turned his attention back to June. "So, June are you into business like your brother was?"

"I'm actually a former beauty pageant contest."

Andre whistled. "Oh, my. I thought so."

June giggled. "Thanks. Right now I work as a pageant coach."

"Come on. You can't be that old."

"Andre," Jemina interrupted, grabbing June by the hand and leading her into Dale's office. "Quit bothering the poor girl. This is Dale's office."

55

"Thank you." June nodded and entered the room while Andre retreated toward the break room. Tabasco sniffed the air and spotted a counter of product samples. Andre sped back to his desk before Jemina could comment on his behavior.

"Flirting with the boss's sister," Jemina muttered. "He has a serious problem."

"What's with the papers all over the floor?" June asked.

"Oh." Jemina eyed the mess in Dale's office. "Well, we haven't touched anything since the incident. Police orders. But I guess we could have cleaned up a little after they finished their search. Sorry about that."

"I was looking for an epi-pen," Mari added, hoping that it would help June understand why her brother's belongings were strewn across the floor.

"I see," June replied. She picked a few things up.

"If you don't mind me saying," Mari continued. "You seem too upset by everything."

"That's life," June said with a tranquil voice. "My brother was a huge risk-taker, and he had made some enemies. I warned him not to make that big announcement."

"You mean the announcement about Andre's promotion?" Mari asked.

"Promotion?" June replied, looking slightly confused. "No. Dale was about to sell Woofles Snacks to an anxious buyer in California." She studied the shocked looks on both Jemina and Mari's faces. "Wait, did none of you know this? Everyone here would have been in danger of losing their job."

"Did anyone else know about this?" Jemina asked.

"At least one person," June answered. "Andre knew. I know my brother told him."

"Excuse me for a minute," Jemina said with a hint of fire in her eyes. She turned toward Andre's desk.

Ignoring Mari's attempts to calm her down, Jemina marched straight for Andre, catching the attention of the rest of the office in the process. She slammed her fist on his desk to get his attention.

It worked.

"You knew," Jemina said with disdain. "You knew Dale was about to sell and you didn't say a word. What is wrong with you, Andre?"

"What's going on?" Yvette chimed in as the room erupted into whispers. "What are you talking about? Dale was going to sell us out?"

"I'm sorry," Andre responded. He rapidly recovered his composure. "Dale asked me to keep it a secret. I lied, yes, but I didn't hurt anybody."

Jemina threw up her hands in the air. It looked like she wanted to punch Andre and was having trouble thinking of a reason not to.

"If it helps," June interrupted, emerging from the doorway and stepping into the center of the room, "Dale's announcement was that he was *thinking* about selling the company. Before his death, it seemed likely that Woofles was going to move to California, but now that deal is up in the air. I have no idea what's going to happen to the company, but you won't necessarily lose your jobs."

"So we *might* lose our jobs," Jemina replied. "Terrific. So, who do we have to suck up to now if we want to stay put here in Texas?"

"Me," June answered.

CHAPTER EIGHT

"And that wasn't even the strangest thing that has happened today," Mari said as she stood in the back office of Lito Bueno's Mexican Restaurant a few hours later sipping coffee with David and Alex. "Did you know *Abuela* has been lying about that sewing group she attends on Thursday nights?"

Both boys shook their heads.

"This is the first I've heard of it," David said with a laugh.

"What else could she be doing?" Alex asked. "Something wild like quilting without a pattern?"

"I wish that were all," Mari said, stirring creamer into her coffee.

She told her brothers about how she had returned to the restaurant after leaving Woofles Snack Company that afternoon. On her way to the door she had run into her grandmother who said she was on her way to the sewing group. Mari could tell by Abuela's shifty eyes that she'd been lying, so she and Tabasco had followed her in secret to the senior center.

"I tailed her into the building," Mari said, continuing her story. "Let me tells you, boys. Abuela and her friends were not sewing."

"The suspense is killing me, Mari," Alex said mocking her.

"What were they doing?" David asked.

"They were playing poker," Mari stated.

She looked at her brothers expecting them to erupt with laughter. Instead, David shrugged, and Alex struggled to stifle a loud yawn.

"I hope you didn't confront her in front of everybody," Alex said.

"Of course I didn't." Mari was outraged at the suggestion. "Come on, guys. She was gambling. Remember all of the lectures she used to give us about gambling and what a sinful habit it is?" The boys exchanged blank expressions. "Really?"

"Why are we mad about this, again?" Alex asked.

"Because Abuela is lying," Mari said. "She's in a secret poker club or something. I'm just trying to figure out why she's been hiding it."

"Who knows, really?" Alex responded. "I've never understood what old people get up to."

"Me, either," David commented. "Maybe she's just looking for some excitement. Maybe lying to people makes her feel like a spy."

This seemed as likely an explanation as any, though it was decidedly more mundane than the reasons Mari had envisioned. But before she could continue, the door to the office opened, and Chrissy came in.

"Mari," she said with an earnest look, "there's someone here to see you."

Chrissy stepped out of the way, and Detective Price entered the room, tipping his hat.

"Forgive me for interrupting," he said, "but I need to have a look around your kitchen."

"I don't have a problem with it," Mari replied, who was already texting her father. "I doubt you're going to find anything incriminating. My dad, on the other hand, might give you some grief."

Detective Price looked visibly irritated. "And where is your father at this late hour?"

Without looking up from her phone, Mari said, "He's just pulling up."

Detective Price seated himself at a small table and waited. A minute later Mr. Ramirez came stamping down the hall into the office, looking out of breath.

"What's going on?" he asked the detective. "I heard you wanted to search my kitchen."

"Well, yes," Detective Price said, unruffled.

"No, it's not alright," Mr. Ramirez argued. "You march in here in front of my customers and demand to tear apart my restaurant like it's some common crime scene. Do you have any idea the message that sends?"

"Sir," the detective answered with an amused smirk, "I could call my whole team over and force you to let me search the place with a warrant."

This was indisputably true, but Mr. Ramirez didn't like being reminded of the fact. "Fine," he said flatly.

"Then I suppose I'll just have to come back with a warrant," Detective Price replied.

"If you don't mind my saying," Mari interrupted, setting down her coffee in a calming manner, "there are other places in town that are more worth your time like the headquarters of Woofles Snack Company, for example."

"We've been over every inch of that place." The detective shook his head disappointedly. "We found nothing out of the ordinary except for some leftover catered food that appears to have been contaminated. Food that came, I might add, from your kitchen." He shot Mr. Ramirez a narrow glance.

"It wasn't us," Mr. Ramirez shouted. "We are not murderers."

"Detective Price," Mari went on, trying to keep her father from saying something he might regret. "Did you know that Dale Robert was about to sell his company to some guy in California?"

"How did you find this out?"

"Rick Kinney taught me a few things about reading body language and such." Mari smiled. "Okay, and Dale's sister told me."

"Mari, take my advice," Detective Price said with a grim shake of his head, "and don't listen to Rick. He's the worst at weeding out liars."

CHAPTER NINE

Jemina came by the restaurant again that evening for a drink. Mari told her about her conversation with Detective Price.

"Did he visit your office again after he left here?" Mari asked.

Jemina took a sip of her margarita and shook her head. "Nope."

"I expect he'll be breaking down the door of the kitchen any minute now with that warrant," Mari commented.

"I wouldn't worry about it too much," Jemina said. "How much harm could he possibly cause by searching the kitchen?"

"It's going to make my dad very unhappy, and you know how he gets when he's cranky. It affects all of us." Mari took a deep breath, hoping that Mr. Ramirez would be out when the detective came back with a warrant.

"I know," Jemina responded. "That is half the fun of coming here. You never know when the police are going to show up, or when someone in the kitchen will start yelling. It's a nonstop soap opera."

"I guess," Mari said with a sad slump of her shoulders. "I just think the police have a much better chance of finding that missing epi-pen at *your* work. That will shift the blame a little, you know?"

Jemina coughed, and her cheeks went rosy. Mari looked at her curiously. "What's wrong?" she asked.

"Honestly?" Jemina took another sip of her drink.

"What is it?"

Jemina quickly glanced around the room, leaned forward, and whispered. "I can't hold it in anymore. The stress is killing me. I know where the missing epi-pen is. I have it."

For a moment, Mari's thoughts spun out of control. She had come to trust Jemina the last few days, and she'd been glad to have an old friend living back in town. But now, she couldn't help but feel betrayed.

"I can't believe this," Mari said. "All this time you've been withholding evidence. Why?"

"I know, and I'm sorry," Jemina blurted out with a guilt-stricken look. She pushed her margarita away as if it was somehow to blame. "I should have told you. I should have told the police."

"Why didn't you? Unless you have something to hide?"

"I think someone is trying to frame me for the murder," Jemina responded.

"Well they're succeeding because you look as guilty as ever right about now," Mari commented. She raised her eyebrows. "I think you'd better start at the beginning or I might be forced to call Detective Price myself."

"Alright." Jemina nodded. "The day after Dale's murder, I was running late to work because they messed up my order at the coffee shop. It took me about twenty minutes to get there, and when I did, Andre yelled at me, of course."

"I guess he'd already decided that he was the boss?" Mari guessed.

"Andre doesn't normally do things like that," Jemina replied. "It surprised me. But given the circumstances, I guess it shouldn't have. He was on edge the entire day, and he spent much of the day locked away in the bathroom."

"So he lectured you in front of everyone, and then what?"

"I went back to my desk," Jemina went on. "And when I sat down I noticed Dale's epi-pen was just sitting there. I have no clue how it got on my desk. It hadn't been there earlier. I thought I was dreaming."

"What did you do with it?" Mari asked.

Jemina's cheeks turned scarlet as she said, "I ... I kept it because I thought contacting the police would paint a target on my back."

"Jemina," Mari scolded her.

"I know. I wasn't thinking straight." She turned away from Mari, unable to look her in the eyes. "I regret what I did, but it's too late for that now. What do I do?"

"What you should have done but didn't," Mari answered.

"How was I supposed to explain to Detective Price that it had just shown up on my desk? He would have never believed me." Jemina gazed out the window. "The killer did it. I am being framed. I just know it."

Jemina looked back at Mari with desperate, glossy eyes.

"I guess it's possible," Mari admitted. "But let's not jump to conclusions." Although, Mari knew that Jemina was in some serious trouble. But she thought it best to keep her friend as calm as she could.

"Ever since Dale's death I've been questioning my own motives." Jemina looked genuinely stricken. She unhappily kneaded her hands together. "What if I *was* responsible for his death somehow? I mean, I ordered the food and ..."

Mari reached for Jemina's hand. It was cold, and Jemina instinctively jerked it away without thinking. She had no idea that Jemina had been living with so much guilt since Dale's passing.

"Jemina, listen to me," Mari said. "Stop blaming yourself, and stop making up things that aren't true. We will find out who killed Dale and who put his missing epi-pen on your desk."

"I want to believe that," Jemina responded. Mari couldn't help noticing that Jemina still had trouble looking her in the eyes. "I must be going crazy. I mean, I can't even remember much about the day Dale died."

"You were with me most of the day," Mari reminded her. "The other part of the day you were giving a tour. A pretty darn good tour at that."

"I feel much better telling someone," Jemina confessed. "If anyone can help me catch this guy it is you, Mari. Nothing gets past you."

"I'm going to have to disagree with that statement." Mari bit the side of her lip. She took a deep breath and tried to push aside her memories of Dale falling to the floor. One thing nagged at her brain. "You know, only one other person in the office seemed to know where Dale kept his epi-pen."

"Huh?" Jemina frowned.

"Yes." Mari replayed the moment in her head. "I went looking for the epi-pen, and someone at your office told me exactly where to look for it. Dale's desk drawer."

"Who?" Jemina asked, trying to come up with the answer herself.

She didn't have to.

At that moment the doors of the restaurant flew open, and Yvette came speeding toward them in her high heels as if she had been summoned by Mari's *almost* mention of her.

Jemina opened her mouth to speak, but before she could get a word out Yvette pointed a finger at her.

"You listen to me," Yvette shouted. "Both of you listen to me good. Stop digging around into things that don't concern you. Quit playing Nancy Drew, and mind your own dang business.

"What—" Mari said, but Yvette turned and pointed at her too.

"I'm tired of the police poking around in my personal life," she interrupted. "I'm tired of being interviewed and questioned. I'm tired of having my house searched. You need to drop this. I don't care if I go to jail, you need to drop it now before someone else gets murdered."

Whirling around on her heels, Yvette stormed back out of the restaurant and into the cool evening air while customers looked on in shock.

CHAPTER TEN

Jemina ended her evening with one too many drinks in hand. Mari ended hers by closing the restaurant, forcing Jemina to eat something, and then driving her friend home.

"I honestly don't know what her deal is," Jemina said. "I would never have expected an outburst like that from Yvette."

"Yvette? Really?" Mari asked as she drove away from the restaurant. "She never struck me as the friendly type."

"What?" Jemina rubbed her forehead. "She's always been the sweetest girl in the office. So quiet and polite. I guess Dale's death is pushing people over the edge."

"Are we talking about the same Yvette?" Mari responded. Her experiences with Yvette had been less than pleasant. "People aren't always what they seem to be. Sometimes dramatic events like this show you a person's true colors."

Jemina contemplated this in silence for a few minutes. They drove past a few street lights as the sky grew darker. Tabasco lay snoring in the back seat, and Mari was looking forward to getting home and crawling into bed with a mystery novel and a pot of hot chocolate.

Mari pulled into the parking lot of Jemina's apartment building. She got out and gave her a quick hug, which she certainly needed. Jemina thanked her and stumbled quietly through the rows of cars to the steps leading up to her front door. She watched Jemina disappear inside, and she shook her head. It was a shame that she and her friend were mixed up in a tricky case like Dale's. Mari only hoped that the real killer would be caught before anything else happened.

The streets were empty as she made the short drive back to her own apartment. Mari was surprised when she saw flashing lights in the distance and heard the whir of an ambulance's sirens. As she got closer, it became clearer that there had been an accident on the road. Two paramedics lifted a slender figure onto a white stretcher.

The victim turned toward Mari, and she brought the car to a startling halt.

It was June Roberts.

Mari parked and got out of her car. Tabasco followed behind her as she tried to reach June before she loaded into the ambulance. She didn't make it in time and bumped into a surprised paramedic instead.

"Sorry," Mari said. "I was just wondering what happened. I know that woman on the ambulance."

"Oh, you do?" the paramedic responded. "Apparently, some driver tried to push her off the road. We have no idea who it was. They had driven off long before we got here."

Mari's chest pounded. A hit-and-run. It could not have been a coincidence.

"Is she conscious?" Mari asked frantically. "Can I see her?"

"I suppose so," the paramedic replied. "We haven't been able to get ahold of any family members. But you will have to wait until after she has been evaluated at the hospital."

"She is visiting from out of town," Mari informed him. "Okay, I can wait."

Mari got back into her car with Tabasco and followed the ambulance through the winding, narrow streets of town. Tabasco was wide awake in the passenger's seat, and he stared intensely at the lights on the ambulance. Realizing that she didn't want to enter the emergency room empty-handed, Mari pulled over at the nearest grocery store and bought a bouquet of daisies. The last register was just closing by the time she reached checkout, but she managed to talk the man at the register into letting her through.

Ten minutes later, Mari and Tabasco pulled into the parking lot of the hospital. A gently beaming woman in the front lobby directed her to the room where June had been taken.

"Hi," June said, rising slightly in her bed. "I remember you from my brother's office. I was shocked when my nurse told me I had a visitor." She eyed the flowers. "Oh, you are very kind."

"Honestly, it's not much, but I hope they brighten your evening," said Mari said, setting the bouquet down on the table. "I drove by right after the accident. Do you know what happened?"

June cupped the side of her head as Tabasco let out a soft bark.

"Sorry if I seem a little out of it," June said. "Apparently I hit my head really hard. I stopped at a red light, and a car pulled up behind me with its lights off which I thought was weird. The car honked at me, but I waited for the light to turn green."

Mari nodded. "And the car hit you?"

"I came out of nowhere," June explained. "The car rammed me over and over again and then just sped off. I was too out of it to get a good look at it."

Mari listened thoughtfully, her head filled with questions. Had June been in the killer's crosshairs because of her connection to the victim? Or had she been just the accidental victim of road rage?

"I need you to answer a question for me," Mari said, deciding to employ the same frank and direct tone that Jemina used when she spoke with Mr. Chun. "I need you to be completely honest with me. Where were you headed when the car hit you?"

June frowned as if looking for a way out of the question. "I'm not supposed to be talking about it—"

"Please. It's really important that you tell me."

"I was on my way to a meeting with Dale's attorney," June admitted. "We were going to discuss possibly selling some of his businesses and properties."

"Of course you were," Mari muttered. "Did anyone else know about this meeting?"

"Not that I know of," June replied. She paused and spoke again. "Wait. There was one other person."

"Who?" Mari eagerly asked.

"I told Yvette Johnson."

CHAPTER ELEVEN

As she was pulling out of the hospital parking lot, Mari called Jemina.

"Mari?" Jemina asked, struggling to stifle a large yawn.

"I'm glad you're still awake," Mari said. "I think we may have found our killer." As she drove toward Woofles Snack Company, Mari told the story of how June had nearly been killed. "Yvette was the only person who knew about June's meeting with the lawyer. She also knew where Dale kept his epi-pen so she could have hidden it. She was also around the time my chimichangas were laced with peanut powder, and she could have easily placed the epi-pen on your desk while Andre was yelling at you that day."

"What are we going to do?" Jemina asked, sounding drowsy. "What if she kills one of us first?"

"She won't," Mari said. "Not if I have anything to say about it. I know you're tired but meet me at Woofles as soon as you can."

Jemina scoffed incredulously. "But I'm not even dressed."

"See you there." Mari threw down the phone, pressed her foot down on the accelerator, and sped off into the night.

When she pulled into the parking lot of Woofles Snack Company a few minutes later, Jemina was already standing at the door wearing flannel pajama pants. She looked unbearably annoyed as she stumbled over to the front door, disarmed the security system, and unlocked it.

Mari reached into her glove compartment and pulled out a pair of flashlights. It would have been senseless to risk drawing attention to themselves by turning on the lights. There was something majestically eerie about the hallways seen this late at night. Mari held her breath as if fearing that the slightest whisper might alert the authorities to their presence.

After what felt like an eternity of creeping, they reached the door of Dale's former office. While Jemina fumbled with the keys, Mari knelt down in front of Tabasco.

"I need you to keep an eye out," she told him. "You let me know the moment you hear anything suspicious."

Tabasco growled low in agreement.

"So what are we looking for, exactly?" Jemina asked as they dug through the contents of Dale's desk in the dim light.

"We are looking for anything suggesting that Yvette might have been involved in his murder," Mari said, who for once sounded more enthusiastic than Jemina. "Anything that would indicate she had a reason to kill him."

But although they sifted thoroughly through his desk drawers, they found only the same assortment of papers as before. Mari wasn't too surprised. If there had been anything incriminating on the desk, the police almost certainly would have found it.

"Have you ever thought about doing this full-time?" Jemina asked as she shuffled through the filing cabinets.

"You mean become a detective?" Mari replied. "No way."

"Right, because you kind of already are," Jemina said. "But having watched you in action for the last week, I can totally see you making a career out of it. You ought to at least be compensated for your contributions to the safety and protection of this city."

Although it was chilly in the office, Mari felt strangely warmed by Jemina's words. She had been sleuthing part-time for about a year, but not on purpose. No one had ever suggested that maybe she could do this for a living.

"I haven't really thought about it," Mari commented. "The restaurant needs me, though. I can't give up working there."

"You should talk you dad into starting a little P.I. firm," Jemina said. "He's always complaining about money. He could partner with you. Wouldn't that be comical?"

Mari snorted. She couldn't imagine her dad ever agreeing to be the second half of a private detective business. "That sounds more like a television show than real life."

"Ture," Jemina said, shuffling a set of loose papers and holding them up to the light. "Here's something you might want to look at."

"What is it?" Mari asked, stepping over the drawers and striding over to the filing cabinet.

"It's a form for an active lawsuit," Jemina responded. "Looks like our friend Yvette was in the process of suing Dale for sexual harassment."

"I'm amazed she is still working here," Mari said. "How much was she suing him for?"

"Not an earth-shattering amount, but enough."

"Huh." Mari stroked the side of her face with the cold edge of the flashlight. "I guess she must have seen an opportunity and took it."

"This would have been very bad for Dale, of course," Jemina continued. "Yvette wasn't the only woman in the office who thought Dale was a pig. This lawsuit could have been the start of many if Yvette had won."

"But if Yvette stood to win a small fortune from suing him," Mari added, "then why would she go through the trouble of killing him?"

"Exactly." Jemina agreed. "Who kills the goose that lays the golden egg?"

"If she didn't do it then we are back to square one again."

Jemina shook her head. "Darn. You were really starting to sound brilliant just then."

There was a brief silence during which Mari heard the distinct rumble of Tabasco's growling. They both turned to the door.

"Do you hear that?" Jemina asked, and Mari nodded, the hairs on the back of her arm rising. Footsteps echoed in the hallway outside as Tabasco trotted to join them.

"Whoever it is," Mari whispered, "they're probably headed straight for this room."

"We don't have time to leave. What are we going to do?"

Mari grabbed Jemina's arm and pulled her underneath the desk. Tabasco joined them looking less alarmed. He wagged his tail as if Mari had been playing a game.

"Don't breathe too loud," Jemina whispered. "And cover Tabasco's mouth."

A second later the door to Dale's office creaked open, and footsteps entered the room.

There was just enough light spilling in from the hallway for Mari to see the slender silhouette of a man framed in the doorway. It was unmistakably the outline of Andre - his hair, his arms, and his shoulders. Mari hoped that the three of them would go unnoticed, but that depended on what Andre planned on doing.

Any second now, she thought, *he's going to come around this desk and find us.*

Mari held onto Tabasco and waited.

Just as they had done, Andre spent a few minutes shuffling through the contents of Dale's desk. But then, apparently not finding what he was looking for, he turned around and walked out the door.

The moment he was gone, Jemina exhaled loudly. She grabbed a file of papers from Dale's desk and tucked them in her purse.

"He was the person I suspected *least*," Mari said as they left the room together a few minutes later. "Besides you, of course. I wouldn't have figured him to come snooping in here late at night."

"Neither would I." Jemina pushed open the front door and a cold blast of night air hit Mari in the face.

"Either he's taken up sleuthing too, or he's hiding something," Mari commented.

"Well," Jemina responded, coming to a halt, "I guess we can ask him ourselves."

She pointed to Mari's car.

There, leaning against the hood with his arms folded, stood Andre.

CHAPTER TWELVE

Mari froze, her eyes darting back and forth from Jemina to Andre. She felt her tongue sticking in her mouth. It seemed clear that he had known they were hiding in Dale's office all along and had been waiting for them to leave.

"Are either one of you going to offer me an explanation?" Andre asked.

"Let's go somewhere where it's warmer," Jemina said, who was shivering in her thin t-shirt. "Please? I can't think when it's this cold."

"Can we not?" Andre responded in a sharp voice. His temper appeared to be rising with every word he spoke. "Let's have this out here and now. I have no way of knowing you won't just drive off."

The two parties seemed to be holding each other under mutual suspicion. Andre could have killed his boss, and the threatening way in which he was looking at Mari didn't sit well. She reached into her purse to pull out her phone. She wanted to text her parents and let them know where she was, but her fingers were stiff, and she fumbled over the buttons.

"Put it down," Andre stated.

"But—"

"Drop it!" he yelled.

Mari glared at him, but she dropped the phone back in her purse.

"Are we actually going to talk or are you just going to stand there?" Jemina asked boldly. She didn't seem as threatened by Andre's behavior.

"Sure, let's talk," Andre answered. In the light from a flickering street lamp, Mari saw the frustration in Andre's eyes. "Let's talk about how the two of you murdered Dale Roberts."

"What?" Jemina said.

"What?" Mari agreed.

"Andre, you've got this all wrong." Jemina waved her hands around. "You have no idea what you're talking about."

Andre stamped his foot impatiently against the cold asphalt. "Then tell me what you were both doing up there."

With a mixture of amusement and frustration, Mari and Jemina shouted over each other trying to explain how they had snuck into the office hoping to find out who had really killed Andre.

"We didn't kill him," Mari insisted. "You did."

Andre's face went pale. "Me? Murder Dale? Why?"

"We were hoping you would tell us," Jemina commented. "What were you doing snooping around in his office?"

"Is that a crime now?" Andre shot back. "Because if it is, both of you are going to have some explaining to do."

Mari saw that this double-sided interrogation wasn't getting them anywhere. Looking across the street, she saw a diner that was still open. A single customer sat in a worn yellow booth, watching the altercation through a foggy window. Mari wondered if he was going to call the police. She envied him for being able to sit there enjoying a cup of coffee.

"So," Jemina said, pulling Mari from her thoughts, "are you going to tell us why you were in there, or not?"

"If you must know," Andre finally said, fixing them both with an unblinking stare, "I was trying to find the killer."

"Oh, whatever, Andre" Jemina shouted. "You are full of it. Why don't you tell the truth for once in your life."

"I find it awfully hard to believe that the three of us all went to Dale's office at the same time, in the middle of the night, with the same purpose," Mari commented. "Do you want to know what I really think? I think you're lying."

"Prove it then," Andre blurted out.

"If you insist," Mari replied. "Your hands are shaking. Your eyes have been shifty this whole time, and Tabasco doesn't like you." Mari looked down at her dog. Tabasco had been giving Andre the stare down for the past five minutes.

"Well ..." Andre said weakly. "I ..."

"Nice on, Mari," Jemina said. She gave her a high-five.

"So let's hear it," Mari insisted, still glowing from Jemina's praise. "And remember that if you lie to me, I'll know. Immediately. Don't even try."

"She can read minds," Jemina added.

"Fine." Andre put his hands up in surrender. "Alright. I wasn't trying to find the killer. I thought if I praised Dale enough, the police would never suspect me. Instead, Detective Price saw right through it. I've become his number-one suspect."

"So you thought you would try and frame someone else for murder?" Mari guessed.

"That's low even for you," Jemina added.

"I'm not talking about the murder," Andre said, fumbling nervously with his hands. "I'm talking about something else I don't want that detective to know."

"What is it, Andre?" asked Mari. "What is so important that you've been acting like a maniac to try and hide?"

"Dale knew but no one else did," Andre replied. "I'm a spy for a rival company."

"You're joking." Mari couldn't help but wonder if Andre, like Jemina, had had one too many drinks that evening.

"Excuse me?" Jemina said.

"It's true," Andre continued, breathing heavily. "I can't disclose the name of the company I work for. Even though Dale is dead, I'm still sworn to secrecy. I had nothing to do with his murder, believe me. That wasn't the plan at all."

"A *rival* company?" Jemina repeated, still struggling to get her head around it. "You mean, like, another company that sells dog treats?"

"It's hard to believe, I know. They sent me to work here and figure out why Woofles has skyrocketed recently. I went in there tonight hoping I might find the formula for the maple bacon treats. I can't go back empty-handed." Andre shrugged.

Mari could hardly believe what she was hearing. If this was true, then it explained all of Andre's strange behavior like his theatrical displays of grief. He might not have been the killer at all but just a corporate spy.

"Okay, so let me ask you this," Mari said. "Who do you think killed Dale Roberts and why?"

"There's no question in my mind who killed him," Andre replied. "It was Yvette. She was the only person, other than Jemina, who even knew where he kept his epi-pen."

"Hold this." Jemina handed Mari her purse containing the files from Dale's office. "Your eyes are better than mine at the moment."

CHAPTER THIRTEEN

The next morning Mari woke up in a world of slush. She could hardly believe what she was seeing as she crawled out of bed and opened her curtains. From one end of the parking lot to the other was covered in wet sleet. This hardly ever happened but it had been cold enough lately.

Local drivers didn't seem to know what to do, and even from her bedroom, she saw cars stranded in ditches along the roadside. But the children, freed from the burden of school for a day, loved the weather. The cold didn't stop them from playing in it, throwing it, and pouring it down each other's jackets. Tabasco climbed onto the windowsill and barked at the happy sight.

Instead of getting dressed, Mari called her dad's cell phone to confirm that the restaurant would still be open. Mari's dad hadn't taken a day off in years, and Mari doubted that he would start now.

"We may not get any customers, but I still want you to come in today," Mari's dad requested.

"Why me?" Mari asked, her dream of lying in bed all day drinking hot cocoa and reading slowly deflating like a withering balloon. "Why do I have to be the one who comes into work on a snow day?"

"It's not a snow day," Mr. Ramirez said, holding the phone too close to his mouth so that it sounded like he was yelling. "I don't care if it got below freezing last night, I can still pull out of my driveway. I'm calling an emergency staff meeting."

There were few phrases in English that provoked more dread in Mari's heart than the words *emergency staff meeting*.

"What's going on?" she asked with a knot in her stomach.

"You'll find out when you get here," her father replied. "And do it quickly."

"Why do I get the feeling you are about to do something rash?"

"I'm doing something I should have done a long time ago." He hung up the phone.

Mari scraped the frost from her windshield and began her journey to Lito Bueno's Mexican Restaurant with Tabasco in the front seat. The whole way there she was filled with a sense of dread. She felt sure she knew what was going to happen. Her father was going to make some crazy claim and send the staff into chaos.

"What are we going to do?" she asked Tabasco, who was standing up on his hind legs with his pug nose pressed against the window. "I feel like the whole town is counting on us fix things. Okay, maybe just the restaurant."

Tabasco barked, although not at her. A brave jogger passed by with a yellow lab. Mari let out a sigh and focused back on the road.

When Mari finally made it to her family's restaurant ten minutes later, she found the rest of the staff already seated in the back office waiting for her. She gave Chrissy a half-hearted smile as she took her seat near the ovens. The only member of the family who wasn't present, as far as she could tell, was her Abuela.

Mr. Ramirez paced in front of them with his hands clasped behind his back. Alex and David looked nervously at each other, neither of them quite knowing what to expect. David looked over at Mari and ran a single finger along his throat.

"I've come to the limit of my patience," Mr. Ramirez announced. "At first I thought it might have just been an innocent mistake. Twenty dollars gone. It's happened before, right? But then it happened the next day again. And the day after that, and the day after that."

Chrissy glanced at Mari. She seemed to sense that she was in the crosshairs, or perhaps she was just nervous. Mari turned away, not able to look her in the eyes. Meanwhile, her father continued his rant.

"I've had enough," he said. "I've given y'all every opportunity to confess. If you had come to me after the first time it happened and told me, I wouldn't be making a big deal about it." Mari scoffed involuntarily, and Mr. Ramirez threw her a sharp look. "If any of you really needed the money we could have worked out some kind of arrangement. But stealing ..."

He turned and looked directly at Chrissy.

Chrissy became conscious that the rest of the room had fixed their gaze on her. At about the same time, tears flooded her eyes as she pointed at herself in disbelief. "Me?" she said.

Mr. Ramirez gave her a solemn nod. "I'm sorry Chrissy, but you closed the register every day any money went missing. I have to let you go."

It was lucky there were no customers in the building, or they would have heard Chrissy's outburst.

"I have *never* stolen a penny from you," she shouted, rising out of her chair with a sudden fury. Alex and David jumped up at the same time, and for a moment it looked like she might attack Mr. Ramirez. Instead, she merely stood there, clutching her sides.

"Now wait a minute, dad," Mari stepped in.

"Not now, Mari." Mr. Ramirez refused to look at her.

"After all the years I've worked here," Chrissy went on, "this is how you repay me."

"You want to talk about repayment?" he shot back. "You can start by repaying the *hundreds* of dollars you've stolen."

Chrissy began to choke out a response, but the words got caught in her throat. This final accusation, evidently, had been too much. She sniffled as she shook her head in disbelief.

"What?" Mari added.

"Detective Price can escort you out," Mr. Ramirez said quietly.

Chrissy and Mari both looked up at the mention of the name. Mari had been so absorbed watching the exchange between Chrissy and her father that she hadn't even noticed the arrival of the detective. Chrissy's expression changed. She looked even more frustrated.

"Am—am I going to jail?" Chrissy asked.

Detective Price shook his head. "Not unless Mr. Ramirez can prove what he is accusing you of."

"This is all ridiculous." Chrissy stamped her foot. "I haven't even done anything."

"It could have been a lot worse," Mr. Ramirez mentioned. "Go on, get out of here."

"Dad, don't you think that's a little harsh?" Mari asked.

"Not now," he muttered in reply.

Chrissy grunted as she left, and Tabasco followed her out hoping for a goodbye scratch behind the ears.

"By the way," Detective Price stated, "I'm not here about the missing money." He held up a piece of paper. "I'm here with that warrant to search your kitchen."

CHAPTER FOURTEEN

Hours later after the detective had left, silence fell over the restaurant. Alex and David stood in the kitchen drinking coffee, and Mr. Ramirez had locked himself in his office and refused to come out. Outside it had started raining so hard that Mari could hardly see The Lucky Noodle across the street.

Mari was seated in a booth facing the window trying to put together the pieces of the mystery that had so far eluded her. Twice already she had texted Jemina and asked her to come to the restaurant for lunch, but Jemina hadn't answered. It looked like she was going to have to figure this out on her own. Time was ticking away.

As far as Mari could tell, she was dealing with two unrelated issues. The mystery of the missing money and the question of who had killed Dale Roberts. She didn't think Chrissy had stolen the money, and she felt her father's attempt to pin the blame on her without any evidence was irresponsible.

As for the murder itself, she had some clues to sift through, and none of them fit together. First, there was the fact that Jemina claimed the epi-pen had shown up on her desk the day after the murder. Jemina could have been lying. It was certainly suspicious that she had withheld that crucial piece of evidence from the police for so long. But Mari trusted her. She had no real reason to trust her, except the fact that they were old childhood friends.

Andre had been acting suspiciously even before the murder, but Mari now knew why. He had been hiding his true identity from the boss he relentlessly flattered. Although not very well since Dale had figured it out before he died. Andre was a thief and a liar, but a murderer? Again, Mari had only her own intuition to go on, and she didn't see why Andre would risk everything and kill his competitor.

That left Yvette. Yvette had known where Dale's epi-pen was hidden and had sent Mari to find it. Yvette had exploded in anger when she and Jemina attempted to investigate the incident, even going so far as to threaten them both. Yvette was the most likely suspect. She had the most likely motive. She obviously hated her boss but why kill him when she had every hope of wringing a settlement out of him? It made no sense.

While Mari sat there with her head in her hands trying to make sense of it all, her mother and Alex came walking out of the kitchen.

"I'm just saying," Mrs. Ramirez said, "I think she's been spending a little too much time with that sewing group. We haven't even really talked since she started going, and customers are starting to complain about the quality of the tortillas. I just can't make them like she can."

"Abuela is old, Mom," Alex responded. "She doesn't have a lot of friends her own age, and I think it's great that she's finally gotten involved in something."

Mari hadn't been thinking much about her grandmother and the fake sewing group. But now that her mother brought it up, a new suspicion crept up on her. Almost as if by instinct she rose from the booth and grabbed Tabasco's leash.

"Where are you headed?" Mrs. Ramirez asked.

"I'll be out for a bit," Mari said vaguely. "There's one thing I need to know, and then I'll be sure."

Her mother and brother looked at each other and shrugged as Mari and Tabasco walked out of the door and into the pouring rain.

***

99

Mari and Tabasco drove through the slick streets of town until they reached the senior center. Just as she had done before, Mari walked through a series of hallways until she found the common room.

The fog against the windows made the main living space look cozy. A bald man with a walrus mustache sat in a leather armchair in front of a television set. A fire blazed in the hearth to the side of the room, and a few women were gathered around it knitting and talking quietly. One elderly woman, festively dressed in a red and green striped sweater, was playing a board game with a girl who might have been her granddaughter. And at a table in the center of the room, Renata and Mari's grandmother were playing poker with four other women.

Taking a deep breath, Mari strode up to the table hanging tight to Tabasco's leash. "Mind if I join you?" she asked.

"Sure," Renata replied. Mari had met the woman only once before, and she had been nothing but friendly. "We'll deal you into the next game."

Abuela looked at Mari with eyes as wide as snickerdoodles.

"Hello, Abuela," Mari said quietly.

"Mari." Her grandmother had a hard time making eye contact.

Before very long Mari had been dealt a hand. Tabasco sat quietly at her feet. While she was staring down at her cards trying to decide on her next move, a silver-haired old woman with a mole on her chin turned to Renata.

"It's a nasty business, what's been going on with that murder," the silver-haired woman said. "Have you heard the latest?"

"No, Bertha, I haven't," Renata replied, her ears pricking up visibly at the mention of the incident. It was front page news all over town.

"It's bad," Bertha commented, shivering theatrically. "Dreadful, really. They're saying the young man was murdered by one of his employees."

"Where did you hear that?" Mari asked. She always had to fight the urge to correct others when they started spouting misinformation.

"I heard it from my daughter when she came in this morning," Bertha answered. "It's common knowledge, young lady."

"It's a bad business all around," Renata added. "When I was growing up nobody ever got murdered in this town, and you could sleep with your doors unlocked at night. The world isn't safe like it used to be. Not anymore."

Mari winced. She wanted to remind Renata that the world hadn't been the coziest of places fifty plus years ago either. But Mari concentrated on her grandmother.

"Anyway," Bertha continued, "he was a bad man. Completely crooked. By all accounts, he deserved what he got."

Renata nodded solemnly as she revealed her hand—three aces and two kings—and took the pot.

After the poker game was over, Mari turned to her grandmother and said, "Can I talk to you for a second?"

Abuela let out a reluctant sigh but followed Mari to a corner of the room where they could see the rain falling on the fence-posts and hedges outside.

"Well, now you know my secret," Abuela said.

"Are we going to talk about the fact that you've been stealing money from the registers to fund your poker games?" Mari stated.

Her Abuela nodded. "I had a feeling you would figure it out," she said in Spanish. "And in a way I am glad. I have succumbed to sin, and I cannot stop."

"You could have just quit the club, Abuela."

"I wanted to play," she said simply. "I like having friends. But I needed money if I wanted to participate, and your father wasn't going to give me that kind of money."

"You could have at least asked him," Mari said. "He just fired Chrissy for something *you* did."

"I've known your father for too long," she explained. "He would never have given me a cent."

"In the meantime, our best server lost her job." Mari frowned. "Who knows if she'll even come back now?"

Her grandmother listened with a growing sense of unease. "I'll tell your father it was me," she said finally. "But you have to promise not to tell him about my poker group. It's supposed to be a secret. I know I can trust you with a secret, but I can't trust my son."

"I won't say a word," Mari promised.

"Thank you," Abuela said and hugged her.

They were interrupted by a buzzing sound in Mari's purse. Tabasco let out a soft bark as Mari scrambled to answer it.

"Hey, what's up?" Mari answered.

"You'll probably be seeing this on the news before long," she replied, "but they've figured out who killed Dale Roberts."

Mari turned away from her grandmother and pushed the phone closer to her ear. "Who was it?"

"Your friend Jemina," her mother replied. "She's just been taken down to the station. Detective Price found out she was hiding Dale's epi-pen and he arrested her immediately."

CHAPTER FIFTEEN

Back in the dining room of Lito Bueno's Mexican Restaurant, Mari read through the files Jemina had taken from Dale's office. She hoped one of them might put her on the path to the true killer. At the top of the pile was a list of all the businesses and properties Dale owned and the ones he had been planning to buy.

"There are several properties I recognize," she said to Tabasco. Somehow talking to her dog felt like the appropriate way to work through her frustrations. "Apparently he wanted to buy the grocery store on fifth, Hazel's furniture store, Bubba's Pizzeria, and even the senior center. What would he even have done with an old folk's home?"

Tabasco barked in reply. Just then the door of the restaurant opened and, to Mari's surprise, her Abuela walked in.

"That's the last time I go out today," she grumbled. "I don't even want to go home. If it means going back out in the cold, I would rather sleep in the office."

"How did you get here so quickly?" Mari asked, watching a red Cadillac speed off through the foggy windows.

"Renata gave me a ride," she replied, shaking her wet jacket and hanging it on the rack.

Mari remembered seeing the same red Cadillac on the day of the party.

"Hey, before you go anywhere," she said, "would you happen to know anything about Dale Roberts wanting to buy the senior center?"

The way her grandmother's eyes reddened, one might have thought Mari had insulted her late husband.

"Yes, he was going to buy it," she said with a vicious snarl. "He wanted to build a golf course there, of all things. He had already given all the seniors eviction notices. They had three weeks to find new accommodations. We live in a small town. Where are they going to go?"

"How did your friends take it?" Mari asked with a sense of urgency.

"Not very well," her Abuela said. "Renata was furious. She had nowhere else to go. But now that Dale is gone, there's a chance the center will stay open. Unless …"

Her voice faded. Mari tugged at her shirt sleeve earnestly. "Unless what? You have to tell me."

"Unless June Roberts decides to finish what her brother started."

Without another word, Mari grabbed Tabasco, grabbed her coat, and headed out the door.

***

All the way to the hospital, Mari cursed her bad luck in having to stop a killer on one of the coldest days in a long time. If she tried to drive too fast, she would end up in the ditch with all of the other poor stranded souls who had never driven through slush before. As it was, she got stuck behind a line of cars and crawled along at a sluggish pace for about fifteen minutes until the traffic finally cleared up.

Five minutes later she raced through the eerily serene and quiet lobby of the hospital.

"I need to see June Roberts," she said to the woman stationed at reception. It was the same woman as before. She looked as if she never slept. "Is she in the same room?"

"No, she's been moved to 4B," the woman replied. "But you might not want to go in there right now. She already has a visitor. Her grandmother just barely came in before you. You might want to give her some privacy."

"That woman is not her grandmother." Mari was gone before she could even finish speaking the sentence. She found the first elevator in the hallway, pressed the button, and waited impatiently as it descended, floor by floor.

When Mari finally reached room 4B, she pressed her face to the window on the door. Inside she saw two figures. One of them, June, was asleep in her bed mumbling quietly to herself. She was wearing a thin blue hospital gown and hugging her arms as if trying to keep warm.

The other was Renata.

She was standing at the foot of the bed wearing a red scarf, a purple sweater, and blue jeans. To the outward eye, she must have seemed the definition of grandmotherly comfort as she held out a balloon, a bouquet of a dozen roses, and a box of assorted chocolates.

The moment Mari saw the chocolates, she threw open the door.

June sat up in bed and looked at them both alarmingly while Renata frowned in frustration.

"June," Mari said, "don't eat those chocolates." Pointing one finger at Renata, she said, "You don't have to do this. You can't undo what you did to Dale, but you don't have to make the same mistake twice."

Renata threw down the chocolates on the foot of the bed looking disappointed. June eyed them with suspicion as if they were serpents placed there on purpose to destroy her.

"After my husband Roger died," Renata explained, "I had nothing left. I couldn't afford to go on living in the house he had bought with his retirement. The senior center was the only place in town that was willing to take me."

Renata eased herself onto the windowsill, and a familiar flicker of anger appeared on her face. Mari had seen the same expression on her grandmother's face just moments ago.

"I still remember so vividly the day Dale Roberts came to the center and handed me my eviction notice. Most men would have had a proxy do it for them, but that wasn't his style. He wanted to do it in person. He wanted to see the looks on our faces when we found out we were being evicted so he could build his golf course. He had no regard for the feelings of others, and when he knocked over Roger's urn by accident, he couldn't stop laughing about it. He acted like it was the funniest thing in the world."

"I'm sorry, Renata," Mari replied. "He had no right to treat you that way."

"I decided to take matters into my own hands," Renata said. "When he first came into my room that day, I had offered him some of my peanut brittle. Of course, he told me to put it away immediately. He said a single peanut could kill him and explained how he kept an epi-pen in his desk drawer."

"What is going on here?" June rubbed her forehead.

"I thought he must be exaggerating," Renata carried on. "But after he left it gave me an idea. On the day of your party, I stayed behind after dropping off your grandmother and snuck peanut powder into the food while you were outside with your dog and your mother was on the phone. Then it was a cinch to sneak into Dale's office, steal the epi-pen, and leave it on a random desk. Of course, I didn't know Dale's sister would come and take over."

She turned her gaze to June with a look of deep loathing. Mari shivered when she saw it, but struggled to keep her composure.

"Renata, listen to me," Mari said. "Don't do anything stupid. June isn't like her brother at all. She doesn't deserve to be punished for what he did to you. She would never have mocked you like he did."

Mari didn't truly know if it were true, but she suspected June wouldn't mind as she was trying to save her life.

"Please," Mari said, picking up the chocolates that she suspected were laced with something. "End this rampage of yours."

Renata rose from the windowsill and snatched the candies away. "I shouldn't even be here," she commented angrily. "I thought a simple car accident would have been enough."

And with a last lingering malicious look at the woman she had nearly killed, Renata walked out of the room. The moment she was gone, Mari reached into her purse and pulled out her cell phone.

"Hey, Detective Price?" Mari said as she watched Renata strut to the nearest elevator. "I've got some good news. You can let Jemina go because I found the real killer. She's at the hospital as we speak."

CHAPTER SIXTEEN

A week later, the weather was warming up. Melting water created pools in the gutters and ditches like it was spring in the middle of winter. Schools had reopened and so had every business in town.

On the day Mr. Ramirez welcomed Chrissy back to work for a private staff party, Mrs. Ramirez came in clutching a bundle of mail in both hands.

"Mari," she said, "there is a letter here for you."

"A letter? From whom?" Mari seized the envelope, although the slant of the handwriting told her at once that it was from her friend Jemina. After the police had released her, she had decided to take some time off.

Dear Mari,

Island life is great, minus that fact that I get no cell phone reception. There's nothing wrong with an old-fashioned letter though, right?

First, I want to thank you for helping me get my job back. Thanks to you I've been welcomed back to Woofles, and my involvement in Dale's case hasn't put a stain on my record.

You'll be happy to hear that June has decided not to go through with her brother's plan to sell the company. She wants to keep it in Texas for the time being. Yvette has been placed in charge of the office, and we will be working to put our differences behind us. She understands that a lot of accusations were flung around in the wake of the murder. It was a confusing and frightening time.

I'm sorry that the police haven't been able to find Renata. I know they'll continue their investigation until she's brought to justice. But thanks to you, a killer was exposed, and innocent people were vindicated.

I guess I'll be seeing you when I get back to Texas.

Your friend,

Jemina

Mari closed the letter and returned it to the envelope, feeling warm all over. She heard her mother calling to her from the kitchen as her father proposed a toast.

"Chrissy," José Ramirez said, "I just wanted to say that I'm sorry for accusing you of theft. I hope you can accept my apology." He hung his head as his wife, Paula, nodded with satisfaction.

It was surreal, Mari thought, to be standing in the kitchen next to the woman who had caused the confusion in the first place. Abuela had driven to Lito Bueno's Mexican Restaurant on the day of their last conversation and had told her son that she had been taking money from the register. But she had kept silent about the poker group, which she still continued to attend in secret.

"And I would just like to say," Officer Rick added, taking off his hat and holding it to his chest, "we ought to congratulate ourselves on another mystery solved, and to Mari here, without whom this town would be a lot less safe."

To Mari's immense surprise and satisfaction, everyone present turned and raised their glasses.

"To Mari," Rick said with a wink. "The finest detective in all of Texas."

"The finest detective in all of Texas," everyone shouted in unison, and the room erupted in cheers.

BOOKS BY HOLLY PLUM

PATTY CAKES BAKE SHOP COZY MYSTERIES
Until Death Do Us Tart
For Butter Or For Worse
Something Bakes and Something Blue
Frying The Knot
Wedding Bells and a Body
Saying Pie Do . . . (Coming Soon)

MEXICAN CAFÉ COZY MYSTERIES
Murder Con Carne
Killer Salsa
Smothered In Lies
Rice, Beans, and Revenge
Crimes and Chimichangas . . . (Coming Soon)

A Preview of **WEDDING BELLS AND A BODY**

(A Patty Cakes Bake Shop Cozy Mystery)

by Holly Plum

CHAPTER ONE

Powdery donuts, decadent eclairs, and flaky hazelnut pastries. Nothing felt more right to Joy Cooke than spending the early morning hours of a new day baking, seeing the numerous baking sheets filled with goodies and then transferring them to the display case. Joy wasn't always successful at exhibiting cheerfulness, but there was nothing that could point her in the right direction like a few hours of baking. She breathed in the scent of a fresh croissant as the buttery layers melted in her mouth and her fingers made indentations wherever they touched the delicate pastry. Some said that Yoga was the best therapy. Joy had to disagree—baking certainly trumped everything else.

"Morning." Sara Beth's voice was sing-song, just as it was every day. She carried a travel mug of her usual beverage of choice – sweet tea. It wasn't unusual for her to sip through quite a few refills as the day progressed.

Joy began arranging scones on a tray. It was only a few moments before Sara Beth joined her.

"Good morning," Joy responded.

"And how are we feeling today?" Sara Beth asked in her charming Southern accent. Her ruffled shirt and golden hair piled on her head like a proper Southern Belle only added to her typical persona.

"Fine," Joy answered, never pausing in her work. "How are you?"

"Oh, honey, do I have news for you."

Joy didn't bother to suppress the sigh that escaped her lips as she looked at her assistant like it was far too early for the latest gossip.

"Listen to this," Sara Beth went on.

Joy did little more than send her a wary glance, knowing that there was no way out of hearing this one. Sara Beth was all worked up.

"The Sugar Room is selling cat and dog treats, just like us, Joy."

Joy's only reaction was to hesitate in her pastry stacking for a split second before moving right along.

"I hear a few people outside all abuzz over them. They say their pets just love them. And they're nutritious too—could end up with their own article in the local paper."

"Who are you, the head reporter for the Gazette?"

"I might as well be," Sara Beth said, lifting her chin as if it were a compliment. "I know more about this town than I care to sometimes."

Joy sighed again. "I just asked you how you are and you had to go spoiling my morning. No more talk of The Sugar Room or the owner, Maple McWayne."

"It wasn't meant to spoil your morning," Sara Beth said, her brows lowering contritely. "We have kitty cookies, but Maple also has doggie donuts. You should try your hand at making a batch of those. I bet they would sell great and they'll certainly be better than anything The Sugar Room can serve up because we all know you're the best. We just have to step up our game."

"By copying the competitors? I don't think that is a good idea. Besides, if I'm really the best bakery in town then we shouldn't be too worried about the competition, should we? And we *do* have dog treats."

"Suit yourself, honey," Sara Beth said around a bite of croissant she'd plucked off of the tray.

Joy replaced the croissant Sara Beth had taken and then lifted the full tray, carrying it to the front of the store. She heard her assistant following behind her, and she could practically hear Sara Beth opening her mouth to go on when the bell over the front door chimed. Any more talk about Maple McWayne and she was going to be in a bad mood all day. That woman had been trying to put her out of business for years.

"Good morning," Joy greeted the couple who'd entered the bakery. The man looked much older than his youthful spouse, and the woman was already chatting about how delicious everything smelled. She wore a polo shirt with the emblem and name of a golf club on the front. Her brown hair was permed in a way that made it clear she wasn't from Florida. No one around here knew how to follow through with giving a decent perm—Sara Beth had tried everywhere before resorting back to her natural, wavy hair, saying that God would have given her curls if she were meant to have them. The man was tall, close to six feet with tastefully graying sideburns and a mellow demeanor.

"What can I do for the two of you?" Joy asked.

"Hi," the woman responded, offering a ready smile. "My name is Fern. We were wondering if you make wedding cakes."

Joy smiled. She loved making wedding cakes, and it had been a while since she'd booked one. Joy wanted to come across as professional, so she had to resist the urge to reach out and slap Sara Beth when she continued to clap excitedly at the prospect of a new assignment to tackle.

"Well, why don't you both take a seat and I'll get pie for everyone." Joy gestured toward her best table. The one by the window with loads of natural light.

"This early?" Fern chuckled, not unkindly.

The most surprising thing to visitors was the downright Southern hospitality that resonated throughout the little Florida beach town.

"It's never too early for pie," Joy insisted. "Especially when it's apple oat. Does that sound alright for everyone?"

The couple agreed and took a seat at the small table near the window.

"Your mother was always the perfect hostess as well," Fern said, smiling as Joy returned.

"You knew my mother?" Joy eagerly asked. She never turned down the chance to learn more about her late mother, Patty.

"My grandmother used to bring me in here as a little girl when I came to visit in the summer," Fern replied. "Dorothy. Dorothy Wallace is her name."

Joy knew the name well. "Oh, yes," she said as she sat down, fork already in hand. "So you're her little Fern. She talks about you all the time."

"She's always seen the best in me. Your mother, Patty, always had a container of brownies ready for Grandma to pick up when we arrived."

"Yes, the tradition has continued, except that I deliver them to her house now. Every Friday." Joy nodded.

"How kind. Thank you so much for doing that. I know she loves her sweets."

"So, when's the wedding date?" Joy worked hard not to look distracted as the tartness of the apples in the pie exploded on her tongue. Adding that extra quarter cup of brown sugar had been the best idea she'd had in a while. Just such a breakthrough was enough to get her fired up to conquer this wedding cake.

"Actually it's a kind of second wedding," Fern said. "We're here for a family reunion, and since I remember coming here as a little girl, we thought it would be the perfect time to renew our vows."

"We're happily married," Fern's husband said, speaking his first words since entering the bakery. "But, my wife's very sentimental."

Fern didn't appear offended by his comment but only chuckled. "Yes, that's certainly true."

Joy barely had the self-control to put down her fork. "I'm sorry, I didn't catch your name.

"It's Ivan," the man answered.

Joy shook the hand he offered. "Nice to meet you. Well, tell me about the plans you have for the wedding so far."

"We want to be remarried at the hotel where our family reunion is being held. It's on the beach. I love simple elegance. Still, I wouldn't mind some sort of reference to golf." Fern chuckled. "I'm a professional golfer."

Though Fern treated the request sheepishly, Joy only nodded in determination. "I'm sure we can create something wonderful that'll work for you and taste good too. With all of those family members that'll be in town, you shouldn't settle for anything but the best. When would you like to come and sample your options?"

"We were hoping to have the ceremony on Thursday." Fern looked over at Ivan who only shrugged, leaving the decision to his wife. "Would that give you enough time?"

Joy nodded. "Definitely. Can you come back this evening? The bakery will be closing by then, so you'll have my undivided attention."

Fern beamed. "Thank you so much, Joy. It really does mean a lot to me that you're going to be the one to do this. My grandmother truly adored your mother."

Joy smiled. "Of course. Thanks for stopping by."

The three of them sat for a little longer as they all finished their pie even as the early morning customers began to stream into the shop.

"May I send you with any pastries or coffee?" Joy offered when they all stood.

"We have plans, so, no thank you," Ivan interjected. He seemed ready to be on his way. He didn't seem as enthusiastic about renewing his wedding vows as Fern was.

"No problem," Joy amended, hardly seeming to notice her husband's curtness. Joy figured that Fern must be quite used to covering for his less inviting manner.

"We'll certainly take something to go next time," Fern added. "I still remember how delicious the cookies were when your mother used to bake them."

Joy bid the couple goodbye and was instantly bombarded by Sara Beth who wanted to know all the details.

"I'll tell you later," Joy said, swatting her overzealous assistant away. "We have customer's waiting."

Joy's attitude did nothing to dim Sara Beth's excitement over the wedding cake. Joy knew that if it weren't for her bubbly, Southern assistant, she would probably succumb to being gloomy far more often. A business-like attitude came more naturally to her than genuine joy. But, Sara Beth certainly helped her to remember to be cheerful or at least smile when she was serving customers.

Joy was proud of how Sara Beth refrained from mentioning the wedding cake for the rest of the day, but she was practically busting at the seams when it was time to turn the open sign to closed. Joy was just walking toward the door to do just that when someone entered the bakery. True to the Southern hospitality that ruled the town, Joy stepped aside to let him in because she would never have dreamed of locking the door in his face.

"Welcome. Can I help you?"

The man wore a pressed suit, had dark, slicked back hair, and appeared to be in his mid-thirties. Joy had never seen him before, and she thought how strange it was to see three new faces at the bakery in one day. However, the irony of what this stranger was about to tell her wasn't only strange but bordered on eerie.

"Ma'am, my name's James Sacks. I'm a lawyer. Are you Joy Cooke?"

Joy's brow lowered in confusion. "Yes," she answered, uncertainly.

"I'm sorry to be the one to bring you this news, but Dorothy Wallace has passed away."

CHAPTER TWO

Joy found herself incapable of words after hearing the news of Dorothy Wallace's passing.

It felt like a nightmare—she and Fern had just been discussing the woman that very afternoon, and there was a batch of double chocolate brownies already wrapped and ready to be delivered to Dorothy's house right on schedule.

"Thank you for delivering the news, but why are you here?" Joy was working hard to maintain her composure as she looked at the lawyer in front of her.

"I'm responsible for attending to Ms. Wallace's wishes," Mr. Sacks responded.

"Yes, naturally, but I didn't think the lawyer bore the news of one's passing unless it had something to do with the will."

"And it does."

Joy's look was one of pure confusion.

"Can we sit down?" Mr. Sacks suggested.

"N-no," Joy stammered, but the lawyer was already taking her arm and leading her to the table she'd sat at with Fern and Ivan.

"I think it would be best," James said. "Can I get you a glass of water?"

Joy only shook her head. "What is this about?"

Mr. Sacks didn't leave her in suspense any longer and got right to it. "Dorothy Wallace has left you a sizable inheritance. Actually, she's left you most of her fortune."

Mr. Sacks was occupied with unfolding a few official-looking documents and missed the shock on Joy's face. Joy's gaze swung to Sara Beth who appeared equally bewildered.

"Here is the amount of money you can expect," Mr. Sacks began.

Joy waved her hand at him. "She hasn't even been buried yet."

"Ms. Cooke, it's important that these matters are settled as soon as possible," the lawyer insisted. Of course, Joy knew he was only doing his job.

"Yes. But I need a little time to think. Could we meet at another time?" Joy took a deep breath, attempting to gather her thoughts.

"That would be alright. Or, would you like me to send you the details of the will that relate to you and then you can contact me with your questions?"

Joy nodded. "That would be much better."

"No problem," James responded. "I know it's a lot to take in, but I will need to meet with you in person eventually in order to proceed."

Joy could only manage another nod.

With that, Mr. Sacks stood. "I have your address. I'll mail the documents to you as soon as possible. I'm very sorry for your loss."

"Thank you." Joy watched him leave. It was Fern who should be accepting condolences in regards to Ms. Wallace. Ms. Wallace had been a dear friend of her mother. Joy and Patty had treasured Dorothy's every visit, though it was still so unexpected that Joy had been named the beneficiary of her fortune.

Joy stood, moving to stack some empty pastry trays. They clattered on top of one another, falling from her clammy hands.

"Go on home," Sara Beth said, taking over the task. Her voice still held shock, but she was acting much calmer than Joy. "I'll finish up."

Joy didn't see any reason to argue. She couldn't get home to her own thoughts fast enough, and she would probably end up turning the bakery upside down if she attempted to go about cleaning up with such a distracted mind. She hardly remembered the drive home to her beach bungalow. Joy mechanically checked the mail and entered through the front door. The comforting meow of her fluffy, white cat, Cheesecake was the most welcome sound she could think of.

"Hi, boy," Joy crooned, dropping her purse on the kitchen table. She reached up, tugging the hair tie from her thick, dark hair and allowing it to fall past her shoulders. The snow white cat stared steadily up at her with oval, blue eyes until she'd removed her shoes and was ready to sweep him up in her arms. Unlike most cats who squirmed when confronted with such attention, Cheesecake gave himself up to it, instantly turning into a ragdoll.

Joy dropped onto the sofa, clutching her faithful companion close.

Why had Dorothy Wallace left her all of her money? Why hadn't she left it to family? It wasn't as if Joy couldn't use the money. The bakery always needed something, and right now the replacement of an oven and the fixing of the leaky back roof were of utmost important. The money would certainly help with that, but how could she spend the money of a woman she wasn't even related to.

Joy pulled Cheesecake from her chest, looking down into his purring face, stroking his cheeks with her thumbs as he shut his eyes. Mr. Sacks hadn't said anything about the events surrounding the elderly woman's death. Up until now, Joy had been thinking subconsciously that it must have been old age. True, Dorothy Wallace hadn't been in any condition to walk to the bakery to buy double chocolate brownies for herself for over a year, but she'd hardly appeared to be at death's door. It was too strange—too sudden.

Normally Joy would have made her way right to the kitchen after work, ready to eat a well-overdue lunch but instead, she stayed put on the sofa. The next thing she knew she'd fallen asleep and was being awakened by knocking on her front door. She rolled over, tilting her head up to listen, disoriented. Cheesecake mewed in protest at her movement which disrupted his position beside her. Since she was in no mood to answer the door, Joy considered ignoring it altogether. The knocking didn't stop. Scowling, she squinted at the clock. She'd slept for almost two hours, and it was now dark outside.

Joy finally swung her legs off of the couch, careful to avoid bumping Cheesecake. The light from the front room could be seen through the window. She couldn't very well pretend she wasn't home. Before she could decide to sink back onto the couch, Joy made her way to the door, doing her best to appear alert. She instantly dreaded her decision when she opened the door to a stranger. The last thing she wanted to do was face another unfamiliar man today. But, unfamiliarity wasn't the worst part of answering the door.

"Hello," Joy said.

"You're Miss Cooke?"

Joy's heart dropped when the man didn't smile at all. He appeared to be in his fifties, and he had sharp features - no nonsense, green eyes, and a strict expression to say the least. Joy nodded, feeling exhausted. She was shocked by the disdainful look the man gave her. He didn't even know her. What had she done to him?

"My mother was even more foolish in the writing of her will than I thought," the man said rudely. "Unbelievable."

"Excuse me," Joy responded, shaking her head. "Who are you exactly?"

"Ross Wallace," the man answered, impatiently, as if giving such information was inconvenient.

"Oh," Joy said as understanding dawned on her. "You're Dorothy Wallace's son. I remember your name."

Ross continued to look agitated. "My mother was old and easily swayed. We'll just have to remedy this situation and put things right."

"Put things right?" Joy felt a headache coming on. She longed to sit down but had no intention whatsoever of inviting this cold man into her living room.

"The fact that my mother assigned most of her estate to a single person that the rest of my family doesn't even know is ridiculous. It will be dealt with." Ross's face was a cold mask of determination.

Joy's head pounded steadily now. She pressed her fingers to her temples, trying hard not to lose her cool. "I never tried to convince your mother to leave me anything. I have never even met the lawyer who came to tell me—."

Ross was already shaking his head, dismissing her words. "The whole thing is completely ridiculous. As her only son, I should be the one to inherit her fortune."

Joy longed to spit out that he was acting childish about the whole situation. She reminded herself that it was a lot of money they were talking about. However, she still hadn't grasped the situation herself and was finding it difficult even to imagine battling for the money when the idea of an inheritance was still so foreign to her.

"I'm meeting with James Sacks tomorrow morning," Ross went on. "This situation will be dealt with in the swiftest manner possible if I have anything to say about it."

With that, Ross strode away, irritation punctuating his every step. Joy took a few shaky steps back inside her house. Before now she thought that nothing could make the events of the afternoon harder to swallow, but she'd been quite wrong. Quite wrong, indeed.

CHAPTER THREE

The moment Joy entered the bakery the following morning, she was wary of what the day had in store for her. Not even the heavy scent of apple fritters could comfort her. Sara Beth had arrived early and the concerned look she turned on her boss the moment she entered the room was almost too much.

"How are you?" Sara Beth asked, immediately.

Joy waited a moment to speak, putting away her purse and washing her hands, tying an apron in place before answering. "Fine."

Sara Beth pursed her lips and shook a flour-covered finger at her like a mother hen. "You're a whiz at many things, Joy, but you're a terrible liar. Did that lawyer's visit keep you up all night? You look exhausted."

"It wasn't the lawyer," Joy muttered. "It was that Ross Wallace."

"Who?"

Joy took a deep breath. She wouldn't be able to spend an entire day without mentioning what had happened the night before.

"Who came to see you, Joy?" Sara Beth pressed. When she used Joy's given name instead of the usual *doll* or *honey*, it was obvious she meant business.

"Dorothy Wallace's son, Ross." Joy attempted to look calm, keeping herself busy with stirring the batter Sara Beth had started for cupcakes. But it only succeeded in making her appear more frantic, so she put the bowl aside. "He's angry that Dorothy left me her money."

Sara Beth scowled. "So he showed up at your house to talk about it?"

"He sure did." Joy nodded. "He said he is going to fight Dorothy's will."

"That is nonsense," Sara Beth said. "Ms. Wallace was in a perfectly rational state of mind when she wrote her will. She was always as sharp as a whistle when I saw her."

"Ross thinks I somehow convinced Dorothy to leave me her fortune. But, how would I do that? Threats?" Joy stopped there, shaking her head and wishing she had bread dough in front of her to knead out her frustration.

"Good heavens," Sara Beth murmured in astonishment. "What are we going to do?"

"We?" Joy repeated. "There's no *we*, Sara Beth. I don't want you involved at all with Ross Wallace. That guy was scary. He practically threatened me."

"Okay, then what are you going to do?" Sara Beth asked.

"I'm going to give him what he wants. Dorothy wouldn't want her family fighting over this"

Sara Beth raised her eyebrows, looking dissatisfied. "But, Ms. Wallace wanted *you* to have that money."

"I know, but Ross is her son. And I'm not sure I want all that money anyway. Spending it wouldn't feel right."

Sara Beth still looked unconvinced. Some would have wanted to talk the matter over more. However, when Sara Beth changed the subject, Joy was more than ready to oblige.

"Can I borrow your cat Cheesecake for a couple of days?" Sara Beth asked.

Joy gave her a confused smile. "That's random. Why would you want to do that?"

137

"Rebecca's thinking of getting a cat. I'm all for it, but I'd like to have some sort of test run to see what it would be like to be a pet owner."

"You talk about the cat as if it would be yours and not your roommates," Joy remarked.

Sara Beth rolled her eyes. "You know how Rebecca is. She's gone with that boyfriend of hers so much that the little tike will practically call *me* mama. I need to know if I'll be able to pull my weight as kitty companion."

"Didn't you have pets as a kid?"

"Pop couldn't stand them," Sara Beth replied. "I've never had a dog or cat. Nothing. Not even a fish. I bet Pop was allergic to them too."

In spite of the shadow hanging over her from the happenings of the previous day, Joy couldn't help smiling. "Feel free to take Cheesecake for a test run. But consider yourself warned. He's a bit difficult to handle and hates change. He might be a little terror for you."

"Then it'll leave me prepared for anything. If I can survive the Cheese-monster, then I can survive whatever Rebecca decides to bring home."

Since Sara Beth was so sure, Joy agreed. She knew there would be a funny story to go with the adventure once it was all through.

When the bell on the front door chimed, Joy didn't feel ready to start the day but knew she needed to. She groaned inwardly when it was another unfamiliar face. "Hello. How can I help you?"

The woman appeared to be about Joy's age. She had thick, platinum blonde hair which was swept up into a ponytail and showed off long, silver earrings and a slender neck. She wore casual, blue jeans and a white, button-up shirt. "Hi, Joy?"

Joy nodded.

"I'm Violet Wallace," the woman said, extending a hand.

Joy hesitated. Violet seemed nice enough, but the mention of her last name being Ross caused Sara Beth to study her suspiciously. Joy wasn't ready to handle another confrontation like the one she'd had with Ross. Did the entire family intend to bombard her about Dorothy's will? Joy gingerly returned the handshake.

"I believe my father, Ross, came to see you last night," Violet mentioned.

"Yes, he did." Again, Joy nodded. She was surprised by the look of concern that came over the woman's face.

"I have to apologize for the way he acted. It was completely uncalled for and not the way my grandmother would have wanted this handled at all."

Joy found herself speechless. "No," she said when she finally gained her voice. "I don't think it is."

Violet thought for a moment. "I trust my grandmother completely. I don't think she made a mistake while writing her will."

Just when Joy was beginning to believe that this conversation might be one of complete understanding with no further mention of the money, Violet asked a question. "Do you know why she left you so much money?"

If Violet had presented herself as more of a threat like her father had, Joy would have been devastated by the question. However, it appeared to be only one of curiosity.

"I don't know," Joy admitted. "All I ever did was bring her a batch of double chocolate brownies each Friday. That's all…."

Silence had lingered for a few moments before Violet extended her hand again. "Good to meet you, Ms. Cooke, and, again, I'm very sorry for the way my dad handled this situation. Have a good day."

Before Joy had the chance to say that she was sorry for the woman's loss, Violet Wallace was gone. Joy tried to shake off their meeting, but she thought of nothing else all day. Which member of the Wallace family would find her next? And would any of them do something stupid? Joy knew all too well that money made people do crazy things sometimes.

Thank you for your support! If you would like to know more about new releases and other fun things, sign up for my author newsletter by visiting my author page on Amazon.com.

Printed in Great Britain
by Amazon